DRAGONSLAYER, DRAGON HEART

by
Isobelle Cate

In Greek mythology, there were five dragonslayers: Apollo, Jason, Cadmus, Perseus and Heracles. Stories of their feats gave birth to legends that brought both fear and awe.

Dragonslayer clans claimed these names for their own. Each clan had one Apollo, one Jason, one Perseus and so on. Each slayer also had a dragon they had to kill called the Omega.

This dragon was the guardian of a slayer's soul.

For centuries it remained this way. Slayers killed dragons. Dragons avenged the death of their kind by killing slayers.

Those who wrote the laws that caused the war between slayer and dragon didn't consider one thing.

That in the midst of the enmity they created, dragonslayers could fall in love with their dragons...

Dragonslayer, Dragon Heart

Saxton Lance—a.k.a. Apollo—is frustrated. He had his Omega in his sights before it escaped into the woods. Now he may have to wait for hundreds of years before he has another chance of capturing his dragon to claim his soul. On a night out with his fellow slayers to ease his disappointment, he is drawn to the scent of a woman he sees dancing at a club.

A woman he wants in his bed.

Orelle Molyneux has had a close one. Defying the rules, she slips out of Havenshade to relish the open forests of Derwent Valley when she is nearly caught by her slayer. On a trip to town, she meets up with friends who invite her to a club. There she lets lose, imagining herself dancing for her ideal man. Never does she expect that when she opens her eyes, her fantasy man is in front of her and takes her breath away.

But both have secrets. Both can destroy the other. When the truth is revealed, there can only be one outcome.

For Apollo to find peace, he has to kill the woman he loves.

Dragonslayer, Dragon Heart

CONTENTS

Chapter One 9
Chapter Two 17
Chapter Three 32
Chapter Four 44
Chapter Five.. 53
Chapter Six 62
Chapter Seven.. 69
Chapter Eight 83
Chapter Nine 96
Chapter Ten 105
Chapter Eleven.. 115
Chapter Twelve.. 121
Chapter Thirteen 130
Chapter Fourteen.. 138
Chapter Fifteen 147
Chapter Sixteen... 152
Chapter Seventeen 165
Chapter Eighteen.. 179
Chapter Nineteen 188
Chapter Twenty.. 197
Chapter Twenty One 210
Epilogue... 215
Acknowledgments.. 219
About The Author 221
Isobelle Cate 223

Dragonslayer, Dragon Heart

CHAPTER ONE

Apollo sped through the thicket, unmindful of the thorns slashing his denims and abrading his skin open. He hardly grunted in pain when a branch drew a deep gash between his eye and temple. His pulse roared in warning.

Too close.

He heard the slithering of the dragon's tail once more, this time sliding through the forest floor quickly. Apollo's jaw stretched when he smiled. The dragon was not going to escape. He had been searching for his prey for too long and now that it was within his grasp…. If the dragon escaped, who knew how many centuries would pass before he could die and finally rest in peace? And damn was he tired. Five hundred years of trying to catch the dragon assigned to him the moment he entered the world was not only frustrating. It was cramping his style. Most of the dragonslayers he'd known had come and gone. Being the oldest of the Pinehaven slayers, the rest of the springbucks constantly ribbed him about his age. His contemporaries had slain dragons and their reward was the long awaited after life. Humans were afraid to grow old and die. Apollo wasn't. A hundred years of living was more than enough. But he had heard rumours of those who did not kill their dragons but fell in love with them instead. He refused to entertain that thought until it happened to one of their own. These dragonslayers, known as the *Feriam* or the disinherited, moved on to live long happy lives with their dragons, until it was time for Death to take them. They were dragonslayers who became mortal men and lived long to a ripe old age. Only when their dragons died did they die also.

It was something unheard of.

An aberration.

A curse.

Apollo stopped, slightly short of breath despite the miles he ran to keep pace with the key to his death. He swore under his breath, jaw hardening as frustration wormed its way inside his chest. The only sound his sharp hearing could decipher was his stampeding heart. He strained to hear once more, his hearing far beyond the decibels humans could decipher. Dragons had the propensity to mask their movements by deadening a person's hearing. By the time their prey realised what was happening, the abomination would have already cut them in half.

Apollo closed his eyes, peeling the soundwaves with his mind, like onion skin from the bulb, each layer falling down at his feet until he heard the exact centre of the dragon's heart.

He smiled, his eyes still closed. He moved his head less than half a centimetre while his ears perked. Even before his breath passed his lips, he let his axe fly. It whistled through the branches, dodging tree trunks with a mind of its own before it hit the target.

The dragon let out a screech of fury and pain. Then it was gone.

Apollo's smile waned, his face a mask of stone. He trudged through the woods, following the trajectory his weapon had forged. Reaching a huge clearing, he shucked his axe from the tree trunk. The dragon's golden blood glittered on the blade and splashed like a paint ball splatter against the hapless tree trunk.

Apollo had his dragon.

But he didn't have his kill.

* * *

Orelle Molyneux removed her glasses from the bridge of her nose and pressed down on the pressure points close to her inner eyelids. The damn migraine was doing her head in again with the millions of jackhammers stabbing the veins in her temples. At that moment she'd trade the executioner's block to have her head lopped off than have to deal with the headache that was ruining the last few days of her summer break before the new term started.

Ara Winters entered the dining room where Orelle had set up camp, offering her a mug that steamed a bog like mist.

"Take this." Ara offered, her moss green eyes sympathetic.

"Will it help this demon tap dancing in stilettos at my temple?" Orelle took a sniff. "Shit, Ara. The food in the recycling bin smells heaps better!"

"Will get worse before it gets better," Ara

quipped, pulling out one of the chairs and looked at the cover that Orelle was reading. "You need to take a break not keep reading with your migraine. Since you're stubborn, you need to take that and it isn't just for the demons in your head."

Orelle blew out a breath stirring her hair on the left side of her face. Ara always knew better. She was the one with a Chemistry degree. But the thought of the liquid sliding down her throat was almost enough for her to keep the migraine for one more day. Taking a deep breath, Orelle pinched her nose before tilting the contents into her mouth. Her throat muscles took every drop, unscalded by the furnace-like fluid. It couldn't burn the crevice of her mouth or the membranes of her throat as it made its way to the acid chamber of her stomach.

It never would.

Just like Ara predicted, the liquid restored her insides and flowed through her veins to strip the migraine before it did further damage. Orelle made a sound of relief as the concoction worked its magick. Ara lifted her sweater and Orelle hissed jerking in anticipation of the pain she expected to slash across the right side of her ribs. Ara gingerly tapped the skin. Orelle didn't feel anything save for Ara's gentle fingers.

"Good as new." Ara smiled softly as she kissed Orelle's cheek. Her platinum blond locks fell in a sleek fountain halfway across her back and swayed once she straightened. "You gave us quite a scare."

"Imagine what it did to me." Orelle gave a wry

chuckle, the memory of what had happened causing her stomach to plummet before an uncomfortable sensation spread thickly across her belly. It was like falling into a chasm inside herself instead of the floor swallowing her up.

"Meredith wants to see you."

Orelle's gaze bored into her sister.

"It wasn't my fault, Ara."

"No one said it was," her sister dragon replied. "She just wants to know what made you decide to leave Havenshade's confines when we have the caves down below."

Orelle stood, her chair catching the carpet, almost falling over her arm not shoot out to grab the back. A huge, long drawn out sigh pushed out of her as she turned away, walking to the French doors that opened to a manicured garden. Beyond was the forest that was part of the property where she could have stayed.

"I needed to run and I can't do that in the caves no matter how huge they are," she mumbled. "Besides, they're not yet done. I'm not a dragon who wants to be cooped up, Ara. You know that. What other reason could there be?"

Ara sighed. "Even after we were told that a slayer was nearby?"

"If you can come up with something for me to drink so that I hibernate when I moult, then I'd take that anytime and won't leave Havenshade." Orelle held her hands up in frustration. "Honestly, I'm so tired. I just want to get it over and done with and give up my dragon's heart." She pivoted to look at the garden once more. "God I hate this human side of self-preservation."

"That isn't entirely human at all. There are so few of us left in this world we have to do everything we possibly can to survive."

They both turned at the voice.

"Lady Meredith," they intoned, kneeling.

Static electricity made the fine hair on Orelle's arms stand. Even the dining rooms lights flickered.

Meredith Castlereigh glided into the room as though on air. Her rose coloured braided locks fell down her back to her waist over her leather biker jacket. Orelle had always been in awe of her friend and more so now when she was chosen as Doyenne of the Havenshade Dragons after her predecessor had been slaughtered by a dragonslayer. Meredith rarely raised her voice if at all, but she wielded her authority with an iron hand. No one dared disobey her and it wasn't because she wanted to keep them on a leash. She gave Ara and Orelle more freedom than any of the doyennes who held sway over their respective dragon lairs.

"Lady Meredith–"

She raised a hand that was white and unveined as undisturbed snow. Her mauve eyes were kind.

"Do you need to apologise and explain yourself?"

"Yes, Doyenne," Orelle answered. A cool breeze swept through the room. The colder it became, the more sweat trickled down her back and along her cleavage. "If I didn't leave the perimeter and ventured to Derwent, this wouldn't have happened."

"I wish I was still one of you and not the person you both have started to stop looking at directly." Meredith expelled a long breath, relief softening her face. "You escaped. That's the main thing."

Both Orelle and Ara looked up. Meredith's jacket was slung over the back of a Chippendale, her braid over her chest. Her gaze fell on Orelle's book of choice and the mug of bog smelling liquid.

"I don't think it will be easy to explain your disappearance to the college if you died." Ara added rising to her feet. "Something to drink, Mer?"

"Chilled Coke would be nice if you have it." Then to Orelle, "College will be starting soon."

"That's why I wanted to relax," Orelle replied. She gingerly lifted her shirt once more. The deep gash was slowly disappearing, leaving a pink trail in its wake.

"Thanks." Meredith gave Ara a brief smile before she opened the can and took a long gulp. She closed her eyes in bliss and sighed. "Bubbles in your throat…just heaven."

"Ugh." Ara grimaced. "I don't know how you can stand that."

Meredith's mouth widened before she giggled. For a moment, she was their friend. The other girl who completed their triumvirate when they were growing up, prior to taking the Doyenne's mantle.

"Good thing we heal quickly." Meredith resumed, sobering. "Make sure it doesn't happen again."

"The next time I might have to go will be a month from now." Orelle stated.

"Make sure, Orelle." Meredith said quickly but the don't-argue-with-me threaded through her tone.

Orelle bowed. "I promise, Doyenne."

"Ara?"

"Not for a long while yet, I think," Ara's brow puckered. "Besides, I don't think earth is my element. I'm leaning towards water. The reservoirs are better for me. I might just take a break and head off to one of the Scottish lochs."

"No surprise there," Orelle remarked. "You've been staying in the water and having baths more times than I can count."

Meredith slapped her thighs. "Right. Now that's out of the way, I have to get back to the Gathering before I get whipped back into shape again."

CHAPTER TWO

Saxton Lance wolfed down his third huge burger for the night. He closed his eyes when the meat's flavour and juices coated his mouth once more. He groaned in pleasure much to the amusement of the rest of his friends at the table. When Courthouse Burgers opened six months before, the staff could only stare agog at the number of burgers Saxton and his friends ate in one night. It was like seeing clones of Shaggy, Scooby, and Jughead trying each and every kind of burger on the menu. The staff never complained. Every time the group decided to grace their premises - that looked like a cantina more at home in the tropics than inside a drafty old building – the till *ka-chinged* the joint's quota of sales for two weeks. Other patrons wondered where the men stored that excess food when their bodies were muscled under those snug fitting shirts that hugged them to perfection.

There was a reason why they visited pubs and bars and ate there. They wanted to check out the competition, wanted to try if they could do better with the food they offered in The Brew Bar they all owned. The difference was that they didn't only serve burgers. They specialised in over a hundred kinds of liquor, and craft beer, the variety changing every day and every month. There were brews that were made from secret recipes that kept patrons coming back for more.

Owen Mann, a member of Saxton's group took a long pull from his beer.

"Anyone for seconds?" Thick brows rose over pale blue eyes. He stood up taking out some crumpled pound sterling notes from his pocket. He flattened the money to remove the creases.

"What a dumb question," Derrick Berwyn muttered before taking a huge bite off his burger, the mustard and melted cheese oozing at the back of the bun.

Owen snorted. "I know you're hungry, bro. So I'll let that pass."

"Two more beers and this veggie meat burger." Braden Adelram pointed to his plate, chewing. He was another member of the group and a vegetarian. He pointed to the burger in his hand. "Man, this is the most amazing veggie burger I've tasted!"

"You can wax poetic all you like. That still isn't a real burger." Saxton's mouth twitched while he gathered the sesame seeds that fell around his plate.

Braden growled. All of them knew his bite was much worse than his bark so they were safe. The only time they became wary of Braden's temper was when he held his boar spear infused with dragon's blood to hurl it at an enemy. So the resto was safe from being trashed.

Saxton leaned back, his arm extended on the table top, his legs spread under the table as they all relaxed in the huge booth they took in the corner of the restaurant. Hunger was a by-product of chasing a dragon through the dark thicket of Derwent. His appetite only matched the frustration and fury eating away at him. He was hell-bent on getting his abilities in top condition if he wanted to kill his dragon soon. His only problem was that a slayer's senses didn't know squat when the dragon took another form: human. A dragonslayer unable to do what he had been trained to do was a badge of shame that extended to a slayer's family. It tainted even those who came before them, a sign that the present slayer had not been able to duplicate his ancestor's exploits. Saxton might as well put a neon sign on his forehead spelling the word 'Loser' to show all and sundry that he didn't have what it took. Lesser slayers slinked away to the shadows. Either they became a shell of the warrior they once were or they became a part of the human world completely, leaving all of what they knew behind. Isolated. Ostracized. Vilified.

Forgotten.

"So where do we go next while there's a lull?" Derrick asked. He gathered his shoulder length hair and tied it atop his head. The lower part of his angular face was covered with a month long trimmed beard. "I hear there's a new bar close to Victoria Station. We can check it out."

"That's close to Printworks, mate. Too rowdy." Theo Rennick had been quiet the whole time minding his food until then. His dirty blond hair with natural lights was mussed. He didn't care to look presentable, not even with women around, as though he made an effort to keep out of their way.

"I'll walk out with you all after three more of these handmade buns of paradise," Saxton said, taking a swig from his pint. The sweet and bitter liquid slid down his throat satisfying his thirst. He just wanted to go back to his quarters, watch some rugby and lick his wounds. If he could get a pad below the streets of Manchester he would. Instead they all lived in Pinehaven, a huge manor surrounded by farmland located in Hope Valley, where hill fog and strong winds kept it obscure, frightening to those who dared trespass save for the woad sheep that grazed on the land. His rooms had been the residence of dragonslayers who proudly died of old age after successfully slaying their dragons, becoming elders of their clan until they were called to their final resting place. Except that Saxton's immediate predecessor had disappeared. He was now living peacefully with a human and rumours had it that the woman had been the dragon he had been assigned to slay. Sometimes, in the middle of the night, Saxton wondered whether staying in the same rooms as his predecessor lowered his chances of eradicating his own dragon from the face of the earth.

"C'mon, Apollo," Owen used his slayer name. "What's one more drink?"

"A drink too many," he answered. "I'll join you until I know you're all safe and sound inside the bar then I go."

"Yes, Mum."

20

There were chuckles all around.

An hour later, their bellies filled with food, the group left the delighted establishment and strolled through the relatively silent streets of the shopping district to make their way to the edge of the town centre. For a Sunday night, the bars and clubs still overflowed with people. The rains had stopped earlier and the pavement gleamed under the glare of the street lamps and the headlights of cars traversing the roads. Saxton cast a cynical look at the cars humping out music while some of the passengers ogled girls walking along the pavement.

"Elections are still a year away," Theo shouted, his hands cupped around his mouth.

Hoots of laughter came from the group. Someone from inside the car flicked the bird, the driver scowling when Theo guffawed.

"Inside." Saxton grabbed Theo by his shirt collar and dragged him into the first club they entered the moment the bouncer allowed them in.

Music thumped underneath his feet. The air condition mixed with the outside air in the short foyer cooled Saxton's skin. Nubile women and looking-for-some-action-men stood at the threshold as though not knowing whether to enter or leave. Saxton could hardly hear himself think, unable to distinguish which was the music's beat or the beat of his heart. The bar counters located on opposite sides of the dance floor were crowded with people who looked like ants trying to get a hold of part of a sugar cube. It didn't stop Owen and Derrick to charm their way through until they had women swarming around them.

"Over there." Theo bellowed, pointing to one about to be vacated by a group. Braden immediately made a bee line for it nearly diving on to the booth. The women who had just left the cubicle looked at him giggling when Braden showed his pearly whites.

"I'm heading out," Saxton shouted back. "Your sorry ass is safe now."

Theo gave him the finger before he and Braden made themselves comfortable. Just as Saxton turned to leave, he paused, inhaling sharply. Amid the smell of alcohol and lust coming off in waves from bodies of those making out in the dark was a scent so pure and innocent, yet sensual at the same time. He looked around straining to smell more of the scent amidst other smells. Where the hell was the scent coming from? That purity didn't belong there. He looked at his friends enjoying the view of gyrating bodies on the floor and pushed his way back to Theo.

"So you decided to join us." Braden grinned from ear to ear.

Saxton ignored him turning to Theo. "Do you smell that?"

Theo inhaled and looked at him quizzically. He looked around and his face cleared.

"You mean the guy behind me that smells like shower isn't in his vocabulary?"

The man in question turned to Theo, his eyes narrowing. He looked unsure if he had heard Theo right, but neither did he pursue it. The man flattened his lips in indignation before he slunk away.

"No dickhead." Saxton scowled. "The one that smells of springtime."

Theo laughed, snorting. "Your sense of smell will be forever altered here, my friend. Every woman here has the latest perfume licking her skin. Hell, they might have dabbed their pussies with it too."

An ugly sound rumbled up Saxton's throat as he sighed with exaggeration. His friend was useless when all he wanted to do was track each and every gyrating skimpy outfit to find the one he'd take to bed. Saxton drew in a long breath, easily eliminating the other scents that clouded a human's sense of smell and concentrated on the only scent he was drawn to. God, it was beautiful. He wanted to keep smelling it for the rest of his life. It eased the tension bunching his shoulder muscles and relieved the feeling of inadequacy for not having killed his dragon. Something inside his chest lightened as though his heart was floating. Whatever black cloud there was above him seemed to lift. He felt something he hadn't felt in so long a time that it had started to feel alien. He experienced… peace.

Saxton needed to know where it was coming from. He focused, more aware of where he was. His gaze sharpened. He wanted to follow that scent to the ends of the earth.

What. The. Fuck?

He combed the sea of bodies for the one who not only now owned his sense of smell but also drove his lust over the edge. His cock was just about to bust his zipper like he was a car gunning down the road from 0 to 100 kph in 6 seconds. Saxton just had to find the source because for some reason he knew whoever was carrying that scent was the right woman for him.

His gaze stopped at a point on the opposite end of the dance floor. A woman with arms swaying above her head was oblivious to those around her as she danced. Saxton watched her, mesmerised. He wanted to cut through the swathe of bodies with his axe to get to her without being pinned for murder.

Saxton moved.

Her eyes were closed. Her movements were fluid, graceful. She didn't need to be in the centre of the dance floor to get his attention. Her arms lowered to her sides, hips swaying, head rolling from side to side allowing her glorious hair to fall around her shoulders. Her arms rose once more in graceful strokes, wrists and finger movements mimicking flames and giving Saxton a peek of her body's silhouette through the flimsy white blouse she wore. She had curves in the right places just the way Saxton liked it. A woman with flesh. A body meant to be worshiped. Cherished. Protected. He didn't mind being burned by her either. She didn't wear any of the body hugging dresses that filled the floor. Stretch dark denims tucked into three inch stiletto ankle boots made her legs appear to go on forever. The dancers closed in, interrupting his view. When he lost track of her, he wanted to growl at everyone to give him a wide berth.

"Bro, the exit's over there!" Owen nudged his

head towards the doors.

That stopped Saxton. Momentarily. "I'll pass this way."

"No way you're going home now," Theo mocked, his voice carrying through the din to Saxton. The group laughed. Saxton didn't give a fuck, too hell-bent on reaching the woman who could have been the only one dancing in the room. Caressing hands of other women dancing along his path made the few steps to reach her seem longer. Two women blocked his way, their palms on his chest. He held their wrists gently, firmly. A brief uninterested smile, his only response before the women pouted in his wake. But Theo and Owen had been behind Saxton and they whisked the women away back to their table.

At last, Saxton reached her. His need to have her nearly made him lose his composure and grab her. He was entranced by how oblivious she was to everyone around her, immersed in her own private world. Her thick curly lashes formed half-moons over her eyes. The apples of her cheeks were plump and flushed over high cheekbones framing a pert nose. Her lips were softly parted, a smile of enjoyment ghosting on them, reminding Saxton of a luscious iridescent berry just waiting to be sucked and eaten. Then as though she sensed someone watching, she opened her eyes and Saxton drowned in the darkest blue irises he had ever seen that rivalled the early morning sky just before dawn decided to replace it.

She stared at him in surprise, her movements

slowing down, and her arms fell slowly to her sides. Saxton raised his hands as though approaching a skittish mare, watching the emotions flitting through the woman's face. He breached the distance, his body now mere inches before her eyes warmed the moment his hands rested on her waist. His thumbs began to make concentric circles against her blouse and the scent that lured Saxton intensified. Her lids lowered but Saxton could see the sensual light bright in her eyes, in the seductive curve of her mouth.

Saxton inhaled and nearly groaned with the ache developing in the pit of his belly. He needed this woman. Needed her like he needed his next breath. His cock twitched in agreement straining against the now tightening area of his groin. He knew that he had to take it slow. He wasn't was an easy lay. Everything in him screamed to possess her but looking like an eager beaver wasn't going to get him anywhere. If security didn't throw him out, the woman might just decide to give him a reason to sing an aria.

She watched him, waiting for him to make the first move. Saxton's grin widened as he leaned down to brush his lips against her ear. His heart flipped when he heard her indrawn breath. He kissed that sensitive area just behind her ear before he spoke.

"Let's dance."

* * *

Orelle never expected to bag a hot guy on the dance floor when Danni and Jared, her friends from university, urged her to join them for an early supper before going to a club. She wanted to let loose after feeling cooped inside Havenshade. Going to a club hadn't been on her itinerary. For one, she wasn't dressed. Second, she really wasn't into clubs to get wasted. The minute they stepped inside, Orelle changed her mind. So here she was.

On the edge of the dance floor.

In the arms of a hot as hell man that made awareness fill her body.

She just wanted to sway a little bit on the side of the dance floor but something made her want to dance seductively. A private dance for someone whose eyes raked her body and who made her burn. Someone who'd hold her waist while she moved her hips brushing her ass against his groin. So she started dancing, a soft smile on her lips. She didn't expect her imagination could be so strong to make him materialise in front of her.

Her eyes opened to a broad chest, before they rose to look into the dark eyes of the man who left her speechless. In her heels, he was still a foot taller than she was. His handsome features looked harsh under the blue lights, enhancing the angles of his face. His hair was cut short at the sides and back. The top was thick enough for Orelle to want to run her fingers through it. Her hands seemed to have a mind of their own as they crept around his broad shoulders, the muscles hard underneath her fingers. Sensual interest rolled out in waves from him and into her that when he placed his hands on her waist and his thumbs rolled over her skin, Orelle imagined the same digits circling her clit.

Heat warmed her chest and crawled up her neck to her cheeks. Orelle swallowed the moan wanting to burst from her lips, unheard with the music blaring around them. But it sure as hell might just be heard by the stranger through the vibrations running through her body. She should have refused, should have stopped him the moment he dared touch her like she was already his. But even as her better judgement bellowed sexual harassment, her body had other ideas. It was just a dance, right?

Yeah right. Not when her arms were already around his neck, her breasts brushing his chest, her thighs against his thighs. Her pelvis…

Orelle's face burned even hotter, lust making her wet when she felt his hardening shaft against her belly. She should have been feeling shame at his aroused state. Everyone around them jumped at the faster sound but Orelle and her stranger moved and swayed to their own beat, lost in the carnal heat surrounding them. Part of her warned her not to get involved with someone she was getting deeply attracted to. She wasn't new to one night stands. She was careful. All the women of her kind had had affairs leaving soon after they got pregnant. They reared their children as single parents. No attachments. No complications.

No heartbreaks.

Orelle had not heard of many falling in lust with the man they went to bed with. But those who did fall had the unenviable task of telling the man the truth. It was why a quick fuck was okay and relationships with humans were never encouraged.

Her mouth twitched, her hips moved against his, enticing him to move his hands from her waist, her hips down to her ass, flushing her closer to his hard-on. Her body was coming alive so fast with just his hands that when he squeezed a point in her ass, Orelle gasped as more of her wetness seeped from her sex. But her breath didn't escape into the air. This stranger who was wreaking havoc took it into him with a kiss that partly surprised and turned her on. His lips were soft, firm, its mere touch doing things to her that no other kiss had done. It teased, coaxed then claimed as though Orelle's very breath, her mouth, her lips were his from the very beginning. The glow that surrounded her dragon heart rippled causing it to stutter. Orelle's attention returned to the stranger when he caught her unawares as his tongue slid against hers. The kiss was torrid and harsh. He was fucking her mouth with a kiss that was best left for the bedroom than on the dance floor. He held her tighter like he was squeezing the life out of her and Orelle didn't care.

The hoots and catcalls around them brought Orelle back to an embarrassing reality when a spotlight shone on them.

Shit...oh shit.

Orelle's body was about to combust but she wrenched her mouth much like a band-aid off a fresh wound. Raw, red, hot. The only difference was that

29

she wanted the sensation that came along with it.

Their gazes locked. The stranger's eyes were just as surprised as hers. Shadow and light covered his face but there was no disguising his dark look that was enough for Orelle's dragon to feel. It squirmed inside her suddenly uncomfortable. Why hadn't she sensed her beast's alarm?

Orelle pulled away but he refused to let her go, his arms tightening around her.

"Please." She mouthed. Her palms heated against his chest and reluctantly pushed at him. The regret she felt made it almost painful to leave his arms.

Eventually he let go. Although the place was warm because of everyone's body heat, Orelle had never felt so frozen inside. She left him standing on the dance floor as she wove her way through the tables, just wanting the floor to swallow her instead of doing her quick walk of shame as heads turned in her direction. The stranger didn't follow and that brought a surprising pang of hurt.

She reached Jared and Danni, still oblivious to her PDA on the dancefloor. They were still at it and Orelle wouldn't be surprised that by the way they were kissing in the dark that they might have just permanently exchanged tongues. She tapped Danni's shoulder and waited for her friends to extricate themselves from tree hugging each other.

"I'm heading out. See you soon." Then to Jared. "You take care of her."

Jared's teeth flashed white. "Always do."

"How are you getting home?" Danni stood.

"I'm calling a taxi." Orelle shouldered into her jacket.

"We can take you."

"Don't leave on my account." Orelle raised her hand, stalling them. "Thank you for letting me be your third wheel."

Orelle made her way out of the club, the night air a form of reprieve from those who witnessed her PDA with a total stranger. Yet she could sense him everywhere. She felt his eyes on her even after he had disappeared in the crowd. Eyes that seemed to want to know more about her than she could possibly give, wanted to see what was inside of her.

Sometimes being a dragon sucked big time.

CHAPTER THREE

Walking along the pavement, Orelle took out her phone. There were several missed calls from Ara.

"Where the hell are you?"

Orelle winced, her dragon growling at Ara's shriek. "Thanks. I love you too."

"Orelle!"

"I did text you to say I was with Jared and Danni. Stop being such a mother hen."

Ara sighed. "After your near brush with death, I can't help be that way."

"Ara, I can hardly change in the middle of the city." Orelle scoffed. She looked left and right at the passing cars before she found a gap and strode to the opposite side of Townsend Street. "Don't wait up for me. I'm heading to the flat. I'll see you tomorrow."

Years ago, Orelle decided to buy a place of her own. It wasn't difficult to convince Meredith about the practicalities of her owning one. It gave Orelle a place to entertain friends without revealing who and what she really was. It was a place to crash after hitting the town instead of having to drive all the way to Havenshade. And it was hers.

Completely.

It was a place she could stay in to mull over her life away from the cynosure of Ara and Meredith.

But not for long, because she still needed them both when she started to become restless. And when she was restless, so was her dragon.

She strolled through the town hall square. The local government edifice had a watch tower that loomed above her. Flanked by statues of local born captains of industry, its windows looked down on her eerily as though it knew her secret. Orelle's heels tapped against the cobblestones reminiscent of Victorian England. There were couples also out on a stroll, holding hands and stopping to give each other heartfelt kisses before moving on. Orelle smiled. Her heart made an uneven beat of longing for that special someone who could be with her for eternity. What would it feel like to have someone not just for a night or a few days where sex wasn't just the only thing holding them together? Drawing her warm coat around her, she walked away.

A group of men spilled out from one of the bars nearby, weaving their way drunkenly along the opposite side of the street. Their raised voices and laughter stabbed the air and many who came across them gave them a wide berth too intent on reaching their preferred watering hole without any altercation. Orelle huddled deeper into her coat, her purse tucked firmly under her arm as she continued walking towards the direction of her flat which was still a distance away. She groaned inwardly when she realised the men were coming towards her. She picked up her pace. They followed.

"What's the hurry, babe? Let me buy you a

drink."

Orelle looked back giving them a mocking glare. "I thing you boys have had enough."

They guffawed, clapping while they followed and eventually encircled her. Orelle stopped abruptly, trying to pass through gaps which they closed quickly. *Seriously?* She glared at them but didn't have the desired effect or the men were too pissed to care. She looked around. Where was the police when she needed them?

"We'll buy you a drink and then you can pass."

Orelle wrinkled her nose in disgust, almost heaving at the alcohol infused air around her. "No thanks. Hey!"

One of the men grabbed her arm. She pushed him back completely forgetting her beast's strength. He tumbled backwards and grunted when he hit the wall of the town hall.

"What the fuck!" Another member of the group stepped up, about to grab her. He was clearly not as drunk as his friend was.

Orelle braced for the tussle. All she had to do was give the men a withering glare and he'd shit in his pants if they saw her beast's vertical pupils. She could feel her eyes burn, ready to unleash the fire inside her but she couldn't cause a scene. As far as everyone knew, dragons were mythical creatures killed by the likes of Saint George. Orelle's heart began to hammer hard inside her chest. The thought of scaring the shit out of the men surrounding her almost too hard to resist.

That's when she saw him.

"What are you boys doing?" His voice was deceptively casual but to Orelle, it was exceedingly sensual causing a fluttering in her belly no different from a hummingbird's wings. Unusual warmth also spread through her. No one had ever gone after her to see if she was fine.

"Get your own bitch," another member of the group growled. The slur in his voice sounded so comical that Orelle couldn't stop the giggle that came out of her throat.

"You think I'm a bitch?" She took one step forward. The drunk jerked when she pushed him against the wall of the town hall. Orelle's palms slid downward. She wanted to puke, the air around her growing heavy with the man's rancid breath. She wanted to hide because she didn't want the stranger to see what she was going to do. But she kept her ground because no one messed with her nor should they mess with any woman they saw walking alone at night.

"You want me to be your bitch?" she asked softly, her voice drowning amidst the hoots of his companions eagerly anticipating a show. Orelle sensed her stranger move. She looked at him giving an imperceptible shake of her head. She saw his surprise but he didn't move any further, his gaze intent on her to see what she would do.

She turned her attention back to her prey. Orelle was more annoyed that she might have to heave the contents of her stomach after enjoying good food with Jared and Danni earlier. Especially when her prey grabbed her hand and flattened it against his bulging crotch.

She watched the anticipation growing in the man's face, his eyes darting at his friends who started laughing once more. Orelle's mouth slowly lifted. Cupping the man's balls she shuddered in revulsion as she rubbed it, just enough to lead him on.

Before twisting it.

Hard.

The man screamed and his friends pulled back, falling into each other in their inebriated haste. Orelle's prey tried to pry her hand away but she just squeezed tighter. He screamed harder causing some of the people outside the bars down the opposite side of the road to look at what the commotion was all about.

"Stop! Please! No more!"

"I thought you wanted me to give you what you deserve."

"Stop. Oh my God. My dick!"

Orelle moved in. "The next time you think of coming on to a woman and assaulting her, think about my hand squeezing your useless junk, you miserable piece of shit!"

"I won't do it again! I won't do it again!"

"What's that? I didn't hear you."

The man screamed once more. "No more!"

Orelle pushed him away in disgust. The drunk fell to the ground cupping himself and moaning. "Be glad I still have the heart to let you piss."

The rest of the man's companions began to crowd her.

"I wouldn't do that," her stranger spoke.

One of the men pushed his shoulder. "You're just one man with the bitch and we're more than any of you can handle," he said his voice slurred. He couldn't even stand straight.

Amusement lit the stranger's eyes, his mouth curling to a cruel smile.

"Try me."

Orelle stood straighter, her body responding to the authority her perfect stranger wielded. It was scary and exciting. Her beast was wary inside her. Intense attraction and fear could be so potent, pulling her and repelling her at the same time. But the fact that the stranger was willing to protect someone he didn't know from Eve warmed her.

"Saxton! You okay?"

Orelle's gaze whipped to the men who approached them. All broad shouldered and looks that would have women melt with lust, they walked abreast creating a human wall. The drunks who surrounded her slowly stepped back and moved away.

Saxton, her stranger, inclined his head ever so slightly to acknowledge the presence of the men behind him. His eyes never left the man in front of him who turned around to see his companions slinking away with the man whose balls Orelle had twisted. With one last unfocused glare at Saxton, the man staggered away running as fast has his wobbly legs could take him.

Orelle leaned back against the wall feeling the after effects of the adrenalin rush. Hand on her chest, she bade her heart to cease racing but it was hard with the man called Saxton walking towards her. She clamped her teeth over her lips to stop herself from being turned on by his nearness. What the hell was wrong with her? Men she had been with didn't affect her this way.

"Are you okay?" His hand was warm against her upper arm. All Orelle wanted to do was ask him to hold her tight. "I'm Saxton."

She straightened pulling her purse up to her shoulder, dislodging his touch.

Her smile was short. "Yeah, I know." At his raised brow, "I heard your friend say your name. And I'm fine."

"What happened?" One of Saxton's friends asked. His hair glinted gold under the street and bar lights. He looked at Orelle, his pale blues filled with concern.

"Drunks," Orelle replied.

"Did they hurt you? I'm Theo by the way."

Orelle chuckled. "It was the other way around."

"Really?" Another friend asked, his mouth turning up in appreciation when he looked at her. He had darker blond hair. He raised his hand in a wave. "Owen Mann. How?"

Orelle's amusement grew. "Hello Owen Mann. Balls."

"Excuse me?"

"His balls. I twisted it."

"Ouch." Owen and Theo winced.

Saxton's mouth quirked.

"Do you always do that to men you don't like?"

Orelle looked at him. "Not really, but he was invading my personal space."

Saxton's mouth widened slowly. Orelle felt the unfamiliar flutter again in her belly starting to traipse down to her core. She was going to be guilty of swooning over a man any time now. She swallowed hard when he approached her.

"And am I invading your personal space?" he asked softly, his eyes caressing her face all the way down to her neck causing her heart to race even faster.

She shook her head. "No. I need to wash my hands." She looked around and sighed in relief at the sight of the Tudor styled pub just across the street. Orelle encompassed them all in a smile. "Thanks anyway."

She crossed the empty street and for the second time in one night, she was the cynosure of stares. She kept her eyes lowered as she entered the pub to go into the Ladies' room. When she exited the pub she ground to a halt.

Saxton was waiting for her. He stood on the pavement with his legs braced apart and arms crossed over his broad chest. He exuded power that she was getting addicted to the more she saw him. Her mouth watered at the sight his body but what mesmerised her was the sexy lips stretching to a wide grin the moment she came into view. Orelle felt like a woman desired and didn't care that women kept on looking at Saxton much to their companions' annoyance.

Saxton only had eyes for her.

"I thought you'd left," Orelle said.

Saxton tucked his hands inside his pockets. "I'll walk you home. Or are you taking the taxi?"

Orelle looked at the number of taxi's waiting several metres away. Despite the strong attraction she had for Saxton, she wasn't ready nor willing to allow him to know where she lived. It was still her fortress of solitude.

"Taxi," she said, the restlessness of her dragon starting to fill her. She tamped it down. There'd be other times when she could take the streets on her own.

Saxton fell into step with her. They both kept quiet until they reached a black cab.

"That was one hell of a stunt you pulled back there," Saxton said.

Orelle huffed. "I'm just glad he was drunk enough for me to pull it."

Saxton opened the cab's door. Orelle nodded her thanks.

"Wait."

She looked at him.

"I don't know who you are."

She hesitated then gave in.

"Orelle Molyneux." Why she gave her real name was even a mystery to her.

Saxton's knuckles brushed her cheek before he

leaned down to kiss her. Orelle leaned towards him, sucking on his lips until his arm went around her waist, dragging her closer to plunder her mouth. It was over just as soon as it began. Saxton leaned his forehead against hers, their breathing rapid. Then he let go.

"Take care, Orelle Molyneux."

* * *

Hadn't it been for Theo and Owen's enquiring looks before he told them to go back to the club, Saxton would have stayed longer with Orelle. Their top of the line security system would have recorded any dragon's whereabouts and would have sent an alert on their phones. He hadn't expected to find someone who piqued his interest when all he wanted was to chill at home.

Saxton walked towards his bike and straddled it. As the engine started, his thoughts returned to Orelle. Unusual name for the most beautiful and unusual woman he had ever encountered. Anyone who saw her would think her features were simple, but Saxton was more attracted to that kind of simplicity of the fairest and softest skin he had ever touched, unblemished by thick make-up or a surgeon's cosmetic magic. She reminded him of the time when things were simple and people weren't so jacked up by celluloid and plastic surgery. She didn't look like an exaggerated Jessica Rabbit with a huge ass and tits, whose body had a problem deciding which direction to fall. Orelle's lips were sweet, her mouth even more. Her tongue teased, hesitating when she tasted him, not like some of his fuck buddies whose tongue slithered into his mouth with the view of tickling his tonsils.

Orelle was what he wanted in a woman. Feminine curves which he longed to explore at leisure. To do so immediately after just seeing her in the club was a cheap shot. She didn't deserve that. His blood boiled and it took all his will power to contain his fury when Orelle had been surrounded by men whose faces he wanted to bash in. Then he saw the unbelievable.

Orelle wasn't the fragile flower a lot of people would probably have thought. It still didn't stop the protective instinct in him to come out for the dark haired blue eyed beauty that was the source of the scent that drew him to the centre of a forest to find the rarest and fieriest orchid. Her scent still surrounded around him and he didn't want to drive out to Pinehaven only to lose it to the wind. It brought a sudden ache to the centre of his chest. If things were different and he was an ordinary man, he'd have pursued Orelle, took her to where she lived and spend the next couple of months dating her. But Saxton sensed her hesitancy and he didn't pry. He understood the need to keep secrets.

Something similar to a vice tightened around his chest. The unexpected thought of isolation and being alone without a woman by his side swept through him causing his satisfied smile to dip.

"Bloody hell," he swore, the grimness he felt

bleeding out of him. He stared into space and saw his life stretch out to nothingness until he killed his dragon. Then he grimaced and chuckled at the memory of what Orelle had done. The woman had balls. Not much Saxton could say for the poor drunk who not only would have a hangover, but sore nuts come morning. Unconsciously, he stood and cupped himself making sure that painful scene hadn't unmanned him too.

Saxton exhaled heavily, starting his trek back home and reluctantly letting go of Orelle's fragrance. He had to stop wasting too much time thinking of what couldn't happen to dragonslayers like him.

CHAPTER FOUR

Orelle snapped the book she was reading for the tenth time and stared into space. Daylight streamed through the sliding doors on either side of the living room in Havenshade. It made the cream walls with its quaint framed pen and watercolour paintings even brighter. She had taken a book about Krak de Chevalier - the stronghold built and garrisoned by the hospitaliers during the First Crusade out of their small library to unwind. She kept reading the same page several times before she gave up. The words were not making any sense when her mind insisted to thinking about something else while electric shots still fired inside her body from Saxton's touch and kiss. Leaning her arm against the arm rest of the sofa, she placed her thumbnail against her teeth.

Five nights ago she had nearly met her demise. Three nights ago she nearly gave away who she was and experienced the best kiss that ever crossed her lips. Now she couldn't get Saxton out of her mind. Even her flat ceased to become a place of solace that she took the first train back to Havenshade the next morning.

She couldn't understand Saxton's pull, thinking that after twenty four hours she'd forget him as she did with other men she encountered in the past. There were men who looked more handsome than him. However, the planes of his face that bore shadows in the dark, and eyes that seemed to take everything around him just kept appearing in her mind's eye projecting it on the page of the book she was reading. Replaying the kiss in the club and by the taxi over and over again. She could easily imagine him as a Hospitalier defending the Krak against Saladin. He would be at home in that environment. And after the fighting, came the time for relaxation in the arms of a woman Orelle imagined as herself. Just the thought made her belly do flip flops. She blew out a sigh. Ara always said she had a very vivid imagination.

Her lips flattened as she stared longingly at the forest beyond the house. She couldn't let her beast out in broad daylight even if the woods were thick enough that she wouldn't be seen. The brown scales of her dragon would camouflage her beast, the colour shifting according to the shades of brown and green on the ground. Her dragon loved the outdoors, loved the rustle of leaves and the cool earth underneath its feet. It loved the brush of pine needles against its face and the sound of forest animals enjoying their habitat. When Orelle moulted, her dragon was delirious with happiness and didn't realise there was a slayer nearby until it was too late.

She looked around the empty room, the silence entombing her. Claustrophobia within the airy lounge raised her dragon's hackles roaring to get out of Orelle's skin. Impatiently, she placed the book on the wooden coffee table and climbed the stairs to her rooms located somewhere in the middle of the manor's second floor. The floor boards under the hallway carpet creaked beneath her feet. Meredith had called in joiners and builders to renovate the house bit by bit. The renovation hadn't reached her quarters yet.

Orelle wasn't a window shopper. She was more of an online fiend. However she couldn't sit still, again. She texted Ara at work telling her she was going into town. Maybe, going out to indulge in a little retail therapy might rid her of the funk she felt. It wasn't as good as letting her dragon slither through the trees and rest under the twinkling sunlight dotting the forest floor. But it would have to do. It should ease the coil of agitation inside her.

And destroy the image of the man who dominated her mind.

By the time Orelle found an obscure place called The Brew Bar hours later, after going through shops and perusing the latest bestsellers in Waterstone's, her feet were screaming.

"Be right with you." The lone waitress called from behind the bar.

"Thanks." Orelle smiled looking around before opting for a booth by the window.

The place would have been more at home by the side of the docks with its tavern-like decor. Save for the bar, all of the tables were glass tops over several oak barrels welded together. Names of places in the world were burned into the scarred wood. Being a weekday, there was hardly anyone inside which was what Orelle liked. She took off her jacket and left it on the table before she approached the bar counter to order.

The array of dishes on the menu made her mouth water and her stomach grumble loudly. She smiled ruefully at the waitress whose mouth twitched.

"That hungry, huh?"

Orelle laughed. "Guess so."

"So what are you having?" The waitress smiled waiting while Orelle perused the list. Her smile slowly turned bemused when she kept encoding Orelle's orders into the till. "Where do you put all that food?" She blushed chuckling ruefully. "Sorry. Tact sometimes flies out of my vocabulary."

Orelle chuckled. She liked the waitress' sassy attitude. She was dressed in black with a slash of dark lipstick that was nearly the same colour as her copper red hair. She wore eyeliner that made her chestnut coloured eyes look cat like. "What can I say? I've got a hell of a metabolism."

"You should bottle that," the girl said wryly. "I'm Sabine. I'll get your orders done."

"Cheers." Orelle handed Sabine her credit card, waited for it to go through. Sabine gave it back with her receipt and her glass of prosecco.

The minute she sat down in the booth, Orelle took of her heeled ankle boots surreptitiously and groaned in relief when she was finally able to wiggle her toes. She took a sip from her glass and stared out the window.

Sunlight painted the day in a glorious swathe of

pale yellow and white. From her vantage point, Orelle saw the pastel blue sky and whispers of clouds floating while people made the most of the sunshine by sitting outside of Starbucks that fronted St Anne's Square. Some families sat on stone benches facing the Square's fountain, allowing their children to play by the fountain's edge. A twinge of wistfulness wormed its way into Orelle's heart at the sight of the pure joy the young parents had for the child they bore together, love pouring into the kisses they shared. All her dreams of sharing a child with a man in her life were in the realm of wishful thinking. How could a man live with a freak of nature? Either he wouldn't be able to live with the knowledge, talk to someone about it, in which case he'd leave her or die when she killed him. Or he would be that very rare someone who'd love her for who she was, keeping her secret safe.

The aromas of food arriving filled her nostrils. Orelle turned away from the window with a smile.

"Thanks Sa...bine." Her heart stuttered. Pleasant surprise brought excitement skipping down her spine. Awareness shot through her so fast that her mouth became dry. Her server's five o'clock shadow enhanced his angular jaw and his grey green eyes twinkled with interest.

"Saxton! You...you work here?"

Damn her croaky voice!

"Yeah, I do." Saxton's eyes glimmered with pleasure.

"Oh." What else could she say? She was giddy,

thrilled. She felt like a woman who'd never had a man in her bed. Suddenly the thought of eating all the food made her self-conscious. "Join me?"

Saxton gave her a lopsided grin. "Sure. I'll let them know inside I'm taking a break. Be right back."

Orelle groaned into her hands the moment he left. Shit, foot in mouth was so not cool. Yet she couldn't stop the smile that pushed her lips upward. The sunshine outside looked brighter and pierced the dark places inside her.

She sampled the fare. The aroma of white wine sauce joined the steam coming from the button mushrooms in the tiny plate, and Orelle's mouth even watered more as the mushroom's flavour burst in her mouth. The other tiny plate was filled with calamari with slices of lemon and a small container or tartar sauce. There were plates of beef medallions marinated in whisky, a plate of croquettes and sautéed prawns. Orelle sampled them all and tried not to wolf them down to appease her beast.

She was taking another bite from the beef when Saxton returned. Her laugh puffed out of her when she saw his face fill with pleasure.

"Sorry." Orelle managed between bites. "I'm just hungry."

Saxton's shoulders shook lightly. His grin made him devastatingly handsome. "Go ahead. I like watching a woman enjoy her food."

Orelle's brow rose. "You." she pointed to him with her fork. "Have a way with words."

"Do I now?" He leaned back, looking at her in

lazy appreciation that made her nipples pucker and her lady bits take notice.

Orelle nodded emphatically before she took a sip from her prosecco. "You'll have every girl beating down your door."

"Every girl?"

Orelle threw her head back chortling before she pulled a serious face without success. "Possibly."

"But what if the every girl I want is the one in front of me? Will you beat down my door?"

Orelle's cheeks were warm as she arched a brow. She swallowed, her mouth suddenly ry.

"Is there a door to beat down?"

The sound of his laughter warmed her. Even her beast purred.

She drained the contents of her glass, the alcohol making her relax. Saxton raised his hand and pointed to her glass. Sabine nodded, returned with another wine glass and poured the liquid into both before she left.

"Want some?" Orelle swept her hand over the plates of food.

"You go on."

Orelle rolled her eyes. "Go ahead. Laugh, cackle, chortle or whatever you do. I like my food. Free country. Go figure."

That's just what he did. His laugh came from deep down his flat taut stomach rumbling up his broad chest. Orelle was mesmerised before her lips split to a grin and she joined in.

"What can I say? The food's good. Join me.

Please?"

His gaze flared with intensity before it disappeared. Warmth as though she was in his arms enveloped her and she had to look down to hide what she felt. Saxton pulled the squid towards him and started eating. Orelle watched him the way his mouth chewed, his firm lips pursing, moving, his jaw grinding the food inside. She watched his throat as he swallowed. Muscled and taut skin. Everywhere.

Oh my.

It was Orelle's turn to lean back.

"What do you do?"

There was a brief pause before Saxton spoke. He took a sip from his wine glass. "I work here."

Orelle's forehead creased. "I know that. What I meant was what do you do?"

"Everything."

"Such as?"

"Cook, serve the food, man the till, do the books, throw the rubbish. Everything."

Orelle stopped eating. "You've told me everything and nothing."

Saxton looked away, his mouth twitching. "I own this place together with a few friends."

Orelle glanced at the bar. Sabine was wiping down the counter while Theo and Owen whom she previously met spoke with each other. Owen gave her a friendly wave which she acknowledged with nudge of her head. Saxton turned around to see who she was looking at before returning to his food. Owen and Theo looked at her oddly until Owen snorted a laugh and slapped the other man on the back. Sabine looked bored.

In a flash, Orelle imagined herself being kissed by Saxton again, to get a taste of him once more. The light mood shifted as though Saxton knew what she was thinking. His gaze darkened when they landed on her mouth. He looked up and Orelle wanted to dive into those cool depths. But the thought of bringing a relationship to the next level was a scary proposition. Orelle inhaled and blew out a breath suddenly unsure. Slowly she wiped her fingers on the napkin, she took out several notes to cover the bill and more. Saxton looked at her, still chewing but perplexed.

"What are you doing?"

"I'm sorry. I know it's rude but I have to go." She placed her shoes back on, dragged her purse and coat and stood.

Saxton stood, towering over her. The vertical lines on his brow stood out.

"Did I say something wrong?"

The please-it's-not-you-it's-me was a total cop out and too much of a cliché even if it was exactly how she felt.

"You didn't." Orelle shook her head. "I forgot to do something. Thanks for staying to eat with me."

Orelle made her way to the door, regret pulling hard at her chest that it physically ached.

If only she had been born normal.

CHAPTER FIVE

Saxton's brows pulled down in the middle of his forehead. He watched Orelle walk away and itched to follow her. His gut told him she was lying when she said she needed to do something and it socked him in the gut. But if she wanted to get away from him, why ask him to sit down and eat?

"Care to tell us what went down?" Theo asked as he approached with Owen following closely.

"I don't have a bloody clue." Saxton's brows were still pulled together. He inhaled Orelle's scent and tried to keep it inside him again.

"But you ate with her." Owen scratched his head. "Then she left. Dude, are you sure you brushed your teeth?"

"Shut up." Saxton scowled. "This is serious."

Owen winked. "So was my question. Okay if you brushed your teeth," he sniffed. "Looks like you showered with onions as your soap." Palms raised Owen walked backwards. "Just saying, the woman might have a strong sense of smell."

"What are you going to do?" Theo glared at Owen then shook his head.

Saxton ignored Owen and glanced sideways at Theo leaving the bar. He strode towards the square, pivoting slowly. Where was she? Why did something stir inside him the moment he sensed her. After that night in the club, he didn't expect to see Orelle again. He had been in the middle of a meeting with Theo and Owen when he inhaled sharply, the smell of sweet pea and a host of other springtime flowers tickling his nose. He left his fellow slayers, intercepting Sabine in the kitchen. When he peered through the kitchen door, his heart stuttered at seeing Orelle.

She was here! What were the odds that Orelle would come to the Brew Bar? Saxton felt excitement that he had never felt before. It was very different from the excitement he felt when he was going for the kill.

Sabine placed Orelle's orders on a tray.

"She ordered all of that?" Saxton chuckled in surprise.

"Yeah," Sabine said grinning. "Told me she had a hell of a metabolism."

"I'll take it to her." Saxton bent down to get the tray.

"You sure?" Sabine looked up in bemusement. "Your meeting with the guys —"

"Nothing they can't handle themselves." Saxton straightened with a wink.

The moment Orelle had smiled in welcome it was as though the sun had entered his body and brightened his insides. His weariness from trying to find his dragon lifted and lightness filled his heart. Orelle's presence made him feel as though he had been given a new lease in life to make up for his transgressions.

Transgressions brought on by his reason for living.

Saxton narrowed his eyes so that people didn't see how they changed. The irises enlarged into pits of coal because it was the only way he could search for her amid the crowd. He took a deep breath. Orelle's scent was fading. Saxton followed the scent. He was no different from a Looney Tune character floating as it followed the smell of hot food.

Bloody hell.

Buskers sang by the fountain. People stood and watched, aiming their smartphones at the singers to film the free concert. Saxton moved away from the Square, into the side streets until he reached Market Street. That's when he saw beyond the groups of shoppers that Orelle was queuing for the free shuttle bus. With a burst of speed, Saxton tore through the square and got to the shuttle just as Orelle was about to board it. He pulled in a huge gulp of air and her scent surrounded him once more causing his cock to twitch.

Orelle's dark blue eyes widened when she saw him.

Saxton leaned down to whisper. "You're holding up the line."

Her eyes turned mischievous. "You're the only one behind," she whispered back.

Saxton felt his cock harden at her voice, the seductive sound fuelling his lust.

Shit.

She made her way to a vacant seat by the window at the back of the bus. Saxton sat beside her boxing her in. His mouth quirked when he saw her blush.

"You left," he chided gently.

Orelle looked away allowing him the pleasure of watching her. Her skin looked soft and smooth just as he remembered it. Her earlobe was dainty and Saxton had the strong urge to suck the flesh and trail is tongue around the shell of her ear before he trailed kisses down the column of her throat. He couldn't get enough of the curve of her cheek, the shape of her nose that tilted slightly upward at the tip and the graceful sweep of her lashes when they fluttered over her cheeks.

"I remembered I had to do something."

He let that pass. "You left without finishing your food."

She smiled at him in amusement. "Saxton, do you go around running after patrons who don't finish their food? Or else uh... I don't know tell them to stand in the corner?"

His guffaw caused a few of the passengers to steal a glance at them. He didn't expect that from Orelle and the fact that she surprised him was a rarity.

"Only you, sweetheart. Only you." His shoulders shook once, twice, his mirth not yet spent. A flicker of pleasure danced in Orelle's eyes before it disappeared.

"Why?"

He looked at her, and he lost his ability to speak. He was a man who planned out everything, thought of every possible scenario before striking. This time everything was a spur of the moment. He wasn't thinking straight and damn if he didn't enjoy it. It was a far cry from the rigidity of living as a slayer that, what was happening now felt like a bright light forcing its way through the fissures appearing on his heart.

"Because you made me laugh."

Her eyes rounded. She scoffed. "That's it? I made you laugh?"

He slowly sobered, his gaze shifting to the front of the shuttle. "I haven't laughed this hard and this real for a long time. I've forgotten what it feels like."

"I'm sure there have been others…" She turned to the window.

"Not as much as you." At that moment, Saxton realised that he wanted to spend all his time with the woman beside him. She was a walking aphrodisiac.

The shuttle rolled to a halt at the next stop. Saxton stood.

"Is this where you get off?" Orelle looked up at him. Was that disappointment he heard?

"Do you want me to go?"

Her mouth moved hinting at a smile. She shook her head. "No."

Saxton sat down again and watched the flicker of emotions on her face and just like that a companionable silence descended between them even as her warmth and addictive scent fed his hunger for her. He wanted to wrap his body around her, run his hands on every inch of her skin and let his fingers sink into her most private parts. He wanted to watch as lust, passion, ecstasy descended upon her and fill her when he stoked her sweetness. He wanted her to lie beside him to rest for it was there where he'd find peace.

* * *

What the hell am I doing?

Saxton had given her a way out and she didn't take it.

Congratulations, Orelle, you've just landed yourself deeper into a shit swamp.

She hadn't expected Saxton to follow her. She had to clamp her mouth shut when she saw him, giddiness pushing its way into her gut and a sweet sensation filled her that lent wings to her stomach. Her dragon purred inside her but snorted too as though unable to make up its mind on whether to eat the human beside Orelle or just play with it.

Orelle couldn't stop the smugness that crept into her smile when she saw several women eyeing Saxton.

"Where's your next stop?"

Orelle nearly sighed at the way Saxton spoke. Deep, melting dark chocolate, sexy. Did the Aztecs talk this way?

"I was going to watch a movie."

"Was that what you needed to do?"

Her face heated up as she laughed softly. "Yes."

"Which one?" He cocked a brow in interest.

Orelle cleared her throat. "I haven't decided yet. Preferably something I can lose myself in."

"I'd rather lose myself in you."

She chuckled. "That's a really cheesy line." To show how she felt she shuddered and cringed.

Saxton's laugh rumbled up his throat and vibrated through her. He leaned down to whisper, his body hot beside hers, his breath on her skin making her shiver with want. "Doesn't erase the fact that it's true."

She looked down. Surely she now looked like a tomato head with her face heating up all the time the way Saxton was looking at her. His warmth seeped through her. He smelled of man and copper, of life. Orelle just wanted to turn and straddle his thighs and rock her hips while she dipped down for a kiss. Her sense heightened at the thought. Her dragon's tail slithered and thumped the ground.

"We hardly know each other," she said unable to stop the huskiness in her voice.

"Now's a good time as any." His gaze branded her and she felt her pussy weep.

"This is madness," she uttered under her breath. She was overwhelmed by the feelings this man evoked in her. And just when Orelle thought that Saxton was going to kiss her, he exhaled, moving slowly and looked away from her.

"Yes it is."

The air between them shifted leaving her

floundering, as though the world had left her boundless in space. Alone and empty. She swallowed past the thickness in her throat, darting a glance at the other passengers, who thankfully were too engrossed by the music or podcasts pouring into their ears. Soon the shuttle stopped at the Piccadilly Train Station. Everyone filed out with Saxton being the last to alight when he moved to one side so she could precede him.

"Are you thinking of coming back anytime soon?" he asked as they stood under the waiting shed. With his hands tucked into his pocket and his hair ruffled, he looked boyish, handsome, lost.

Orelle stood uncertainly looking around but at him. People strode briskly into the station, some nearly bumping each other in their haste.

"I might," she said still not understanding why a void opened in the centre of her being the moment he moved away.

Saxton's lips curved upwards, his dimple showing. "Drop by the Brew Bar the next time you're back. It'll be on the house." He winked then he was gone, turning away to walk back where he came from until Orelle could no longer see him.

She entered the station deep in thought unable to contain the sadness inside her. Her eyes misted over causing her to suck in a huge breath. She blinked the moisture away looking around to force her mind to think of something else and not the man who had just left. Hugging her purse closer to her chest, she veered away to the left exit of the station, striding to the parking lot. This time she couldn't wait to get home.

Away from Saxton.

CHAPTER SIX

Apollo scoured the forest woods, returning to where he had last seen his dragon. Cadmus and Jason trudged behind him, their swords locked behind their backs. In the dim light of the moon that winked through the trees densely covering Hope Valley, the dragonslayers picked the ground for clues to where Apollo's dragon could be hiding. In the distance, they could hear the waters of the Ladybower, Derwent, and Howden, the water lapping against the smooth stones and sand. Eventually they came to the tree that still had the remnants of the dragon's blood. It shimmered like some extraordinary sap that would eventually turn into rare golden amber.

"Your dragon has evolved." Jason's eyes narrowed at the trunk about to touch the dried blood.

"Don't," Apollo growled low, anger glowing inside him until it consumed him.

Jason eyed him with derision. "You do know we're immune."

"Yes." Apollo jerked his head in a nod.

"So where's that coming from?" Cadmus stood beside Jason looking at Apollo quizzically.

"I don't know." Apollo looked away unable to understand this possessiveness over his dragon's spilled blood. "Your guess is as good as mine."

"Let's split up." Cadmus moved away. "We'll be able to cover more ground. Apollo?"

"Right behind you."

"Staring at the trunk isn't going to bring your dragon back." Jason mocked. "It would be stupid enough to do so knowing a blade is waiting for it."

Apollo had one ear on what Jason said and his attention on the blood splattered tree. There was something familiar and it wasn't just about the blood. It had more to do with its very essence he couldn't put a finger on. The truth teased around the edges of his mind refusing to come to the fore. Apollo knew he was deeply connected to his dragon because of his missing soul but wanting to possess even the dragon's spilled blood? He didn't even feel any possessiveness to end its life the moment his axe connected with his dragon the first time. What happened between then and now? The same vice like grip around his chest took hold of him. This time it squeezed every crevice inside him as though killing his dragon was going to be his own personal tragedy, not his sought after victory.

He couldn't breathe. He inhaled and it was painful, like his lungs were being whipped and his ribs broken. Agony. As though his heart was about to break open. He staggered back falling to his knees.

"Apollo!"

Jason's voice sounded as though it was coming from underwater. Apollo looked up, his blurry vision taking in the silhouette of his brother slayer. Oh fuck, he was going pass out. He couldn't let that happen.

Heracles would never let him live it down. With a growl he surged forward, his hand clawing the bark to get rid of the dragon's blood.

Suddenly his lungs cleared and he fed air into them. The remorse that filled his body slid away like syrup running down the sides of a glass jar. His heartbeat thudded loud in his ears.

What the fuck just happen?

A set of boots entered his line of vision. Apollo glanced up.

"What the hell happened to you?" Cadmus asked, his brow wrinkling. He extended an arm and hauled Apollo to his feet. Apollo looked at his hand where part of the bark with traces of the dragon's blood dotted his palm.

"I have no idea. This blood must really be powerful," he muttered.

Cadmus turned his palm up, peering into it. "Doesn't look like you got burned."

Apollo grunted. He wasn't worried about being burned. Wounds healed. He was more at a loss about his feelings for the creature that made his long life a living hell when he should already been sleeping in eternal repose. He was five hundred years old and without an end in sight to his long existence. Shutting down all emotions inside him, Apollo focused on tracking his dragon. His strong sense of smell separated the earthy musk of dead leaves and mud and from the resin oozing out from some of the trees surrounding them. With superhuman eyesight they were gifted with, they scoured the ground. Apollo watched an earthworm struggle on the forest bed, trying to find shelter against the elements by slithering between the leaves before burrowing itself to safety. He looked around. Cadmus and Jason covered the ground to his left and right.

Apollo's jaw ticked. He had to find his dragon. His clan had been waiting for him to relinquish the helm and let others take their rightful place as the next dragonslayer with his slayer name. He couldn't let them down. He refused to even entertain the thought. During the Huge Convening, many of the slayers were two centuries younger than he was. Jason and Cadmus were also getting on in years but they were still a century or so younger. Still they had their amount of ribbing from the young turks. His contemporaries were all gone save for one whose name Apollo refused to utter. This dragonslayer had brought shame to his own clan until his name and memory were removed from the clan's records and oral history. His name: Perseus of the Rhodes.

Apollo and Perseus had trained together, joining the armies that killed dragons before they were given their Omegas, their final dragons that would give them glory and establish their legends among future dragonslayers. He had been with Perseus when they first saw Perseus' Omega off the cliffs of Dover. They left their hard ridden, puffing steeds several feet away from the cliffs and crawled on their bellies to peer down. The dragon hadn't heard them, too intent on cleaning itself amid the roar of the waves lashing against the rocks. It was a winged serpent whose scales changed from silver to light blue every time it moved. Its talons were sharp enough to pierce the soil and the boulder where it rested. Along its back were horns in decreasing size ending in a long one at the tip of its tail. The point of the horn had the venom equivalent to a hundred scorpions. Its silvery blue hair started from its topmost horn to half way down its back. It reminded Apollo of the kelpie, the mythical Scottish horse-like creatures that lured unsuspecting humans to the loch's deep never to be seen again.

Saxton had watched the zeal fill his friend's eyes as they eased back and stood. Perseus held a battle axe in each hand, his eyes never leaving his quarry.

"I can feel it, Apollo. I can finally fill the void."

Apollo chuckled. He sank his broadsword on the rocky ground and leaned on it.

"I envy you, my friend. Peace is not far away."

Perseus had charged at the dragon, flying through the air in his armour. The dragon let out a piercing scream of anguish when the slayer's axes hit the sides of its neck. Its head moved violently from side to side trying to throw the slayer out of its back. Perseus held fast. His Omega flew high, its wings flapping in indignation before it dove into the sea, taking Perseus with it.

In the end, Perseus' name had been whispered with disgust and shame until he wasn't spoken of anymore. At first Apollo refused to believe the impossible but the more evidence was shown to him about Perseus, he had to admit that it was impossible for the proof to have been fabricated. It had broken Apollo's heart but increased his hatred a hundred fold for the slayer he had called brother and friend. Perseus had defied all that he had been taught and had given up all that he had ever known.

By falling in love with his dragon.

The rustling sound of leaves on the forest floor and the wind cooling the sweat off his neck brought Apollo back to the present, his gaze sharpening and returning the painful memory back into the deep recesses of his mind. He crunched the growth underneath his boot including the earthworm's body wriggling and flattened beneath the leaf it sought shelter from.

What happened to Perseus was not going to happen to him. Dragons had to be eradicated from the world or it would lay destruction in its wake. It was also the key to his glory. Apollo needed to get that piece held ransom by the dragon.

If he wanted to be at peace with himself.

The slayers walked over much of the forest, breaking apart and regrouping until the bluish tint of dawn encroached upon the night sky. There was no sign of Apollo's dragon slithering through the thicket until they reached a natural rock formation that looked like a giant's sculpture studio left to the elements. The rock surface on both sides of the narrow path was dotted with moss that gave it an ethereal green sheen. Tree branches from lichen covered trees pushed out from cracks where tree roots had dug deep. By the time the slayers called it a night, the sky was beginning to lighten and the temperature had dropped.

"We'll come back next time." Jason clamped Apollo on the shoulder, his face filled with empathy.

Apollo's face hardened. The next time his dragon appeared he was going to make damn sure he wasn't going to miss.

CHAPTER SEVEN

Saxton was in the office looking at the accounts when he heard a knock on the door before Sabine peered inside.

"You've got a visitor."

"Who?" He didn't bother looking up.

"Dunno. Some guy. Said he knows you very well."

Saxton looked up, the frown of concentration turning into a scowl. "Get his number. I'll call later." It was freaking middle of the day, a lull in the arrival of customers, and the best time to look at the accounts.

That was what he kept saying to himself. He was getting irritated, unable to concentrate on the books when Orelle was all he could think of. All his boner thought of. He had let go in the shower early that morning but his hand was nothing compared to the thought of sinking into her, to hear her release, feel her nails raking his back with welts until they both came. And he'd still continue to be buried inside her. He groaned inwardly refusing to let Sabine see his discomfort under the table. It had been a week since their shuttle ride and he had no bloody clue where Orelle was or where she lived. Just as he was able to focus on the accounts, Sabine interrupted him.

A lot of people called and knew him. Aside from taking care of the accounting side of the bar, Saxton brokered business introductions. He placed people in touch with each other who went into business together. He never asked for a commission. They gave it to him, afraid that if they didn't their business transactions would sour.

"I don't think he's any of the shysters you normally deal with," Sabine quipped. "Deal with it." She left the door open.

Hurling his pen on the table Saxton followed her out, scowling. Sabine could be a damned nuisance even if she was the best bouncer they had. His footsteps resounded on the wooden floor before they faltered when he inhaled his past drifting towards him. Some sort of a truce. Saxton staggered back like he had been punched in the gut. The sound of plates being dunked into the sink to be washed and the loud voice of their chef reminiscing about the restaurants he used to work in blurred in the wake of the rush of blood in Saxton's ears. His face hardened, rage surging through his system. He was having difficulty keeping his fury on a leash. He stood against the wall, eyes boring into the cracks of the ceiling that had to be repaired, watching some of the cobwebs that had escaped their cleaner's eye sway with every whiff of breeze passing through.

Sabine returned, a growing frown on her forehead.

"Sax…" She faltered when he glared at her. Her frown cleared and she nodded. "I'll ask him to leave."

Saxton looked over Sabine to the man who stared at him. The man's slight smile of greeting wavered under Saxton's fury. So his mouth drooped to a line instead. With an imperceptible nod, the man stood.

"Tell him to wait," Saxton snapped, then in a calmer voice. "I'll be there in a minute."

Sabine pivoted towards the visitor speaking to him in hushed tones. The visitor hesitated before he nodded and sat back down. Sabine moved away with a smile to seat two men in a cubicle by the window in the relatively empty bar. Pulling every ounce of patience he had, Saxton's pace was laid back as he approached the table.

Unlike the anger roaring for blood inside his chest.

"Didn't think you'd still be alive." Saxton eyed the man with dark eyes and ash grey hair. As broad shouldered and muscled as Saxton, he hadn't aged. What he did have was a calmer demeanour than when Saxton last saw him.

"Take a seat, Saxton." The visitor offered the other chair across from him. He was very much at ease and unfazed by Saxton's anger. "I was expecting you wouldn't see me. I was just leaving."

"You shouldn't even have come in the first place. Would have saved me from telling Sabine not to let you stay. Didn't want her to know what a traitor you are."

A flash of pain flit through the stranger's face

before he stood.

"Sit the fuck down." Saxton hissed.

The stranger grimaced. "Peace Saxton. I didn't come here to fight."

"Doubt if you still have it in you, Ty."

His chin lowered to his head before letting out a mirthless chuckle.

"It doesn't look like you're going to listen." Ty's tone was clipped.

Saxton closed the distance between them.

"When I tell you to sit the fuck down, I mean sit the fuck down," he seethed.

Ty's relaxed demeanour disappeared, replaced by ice that Saxton knew so well.

"You have no authority over me Lance," Ty said calling Saxton by his last name. "Never have. Never will." Ty took his light jacket from the back of the chair. "Be careful, Apollo. Your time has come."

"What's that supposed to mean?"

Ty took out a calling card from his jacket pocket and threw it on the table. "That is what it's supposed to mean."

Saxton glanced at it. "Greenisle."

"I've become a better man because of that place. In the end you're going to need it."

Saxton's lip curled. "Don't think so. Looks like a place for lesser men."

The fury in Ty's dark eyes was one Saxton remembered that made ordinary men quake in their skin. It was Ty's turn to close in on Saxton.

"I can still take you down and your sorry face

will fall in love with the ground for good," he said. "Be glad I'm not in a fighting mood right now. And FYI, I didn't want to be here." Ty shoved his shoulder at Saxton causing him to stagger back.

"Then why did you?"

Ty stopped mid-stride, his hands balled into fists.

"Because Lia sent me." He threw over his shoulder before he pushed the door of the bar that it slammed against the wall.

Cold rage filled Saxton. He wanted to smash something. Hell, he wanted to tear down the bar. He looked away. He was no different from Ty and that was the last thing he wanted to happen.

A small but strong hand wrapped over his bicep and turned him around.

"What the hell, Sax?"

"Stay the hell out of my business, Sabine."

Sabine stiffened, her eyes flashing black fire. "Well excuse me, asshole. In case you've forgotten, the bar is my business. So next time you start shouting at the customer? Make sure the bar's empty. Otherwise, take it outside."

"He wasn't a customer," he said and it rankled when Sabine chortled.

"Could have fooled me. Bought a pint and downed it or didn't you even see it because your head was up where the sun don't shine." She picked up something from the table and slammed it hard against Saxton's wall of a chest. "Here. Don't leave your angst where everyone can see it." She stormed off.

"Sabine!"

She continued towards the bar, flicking the bird at him.

Saxton raked his fingers through his hair, stopping midway when he espied the two men who darted a glance at him before going back to their conversation. He strode back to his office, slamming the door behind him. His pent up anger doubled when he belatedly realized the door only closed slowly and softly. He felt caged in, his long strides taking him from one side of the room to the other in just four long steps. With a growl he grabbed his jacket from the couch by the side of the door and left by the back door.

The day had turned from gloriously sunny to abysmally rainy. The building didn't have any overhang and the rain eagerly pelted him the moment he stepped out. Saxton sidestepped the communal refuse bin and potholes gouged like pockmarks on the cobblestones. People walked past the alley he emerged from, umbrellas of all sizes and designs unfurled. Waiting for a family to pass, Saxton veered left and away from the centre to Castlefield and made his way to the ruins of the Roman fort. Hardly anyone was in the area. The lush greenery of the gardens contrasted with the millennia old wall that symbolised Rome's dominion over Britannia. Saxton looked at the wall. If the stones could talk there'd be a lot to learn about the lives of the fallen and the secrets they brought to their graves. Of legends passed on to them by the people they conquered and brought to heel. He wondered whether any of the men had seen dragons flying in the skies of a fledgling nation or if even the mightiest of Rome's generals cowered in the face of the winged demon.

Rain watered his leather jacket, made jagged marks on his denims and started to plaster his dark hair on to his head. Tousling the wetness off, he looked around. A tour coach slowed to a halt in front of the Museum of Science and Industry. The soft tones of tourists speaking followed the pressurised opening of the coach's door.

And the faint scent of a meadow's sweetness after a gentle rain that had him hardening in his pants once more.

Orelle?

Saxton crossed the street, water splashing under his boots in his haste to get to the museum's entrance. The moment he passed the coach his lips widened to a satisfied grin.

* * *

Orelle ducked into the coffee shop the moment the heavens decided to cry over the sunny day and pour its weight down on hapless humans.

"So much for listening to the weather report," she muttered, sighing.

Getting a mug of skinny latte from the counter, she found a table by the far corner of the café. She squinted at the rain from the confines of the café's glass walls before surveying her surroundings. The café looked like an industrial cantina with exposed pipes and vents overhead. Vacant chrome and wood tables filled up as tourists from the coach that had just arrived formed a line at the counter. The din multiplied as chairs were pulled out and scrapped the floor.

Orelle cupped her mug and exhaled gratefully as the intense heat of her scalding beverage seeped through her icy fingers. Her lips thinned. Soon it would become icy hands and frozen feet. Next she'd be shivering for no reason. A sign that she'd have to moult.

Again.

She shuddered at the memory of the last time she took her dragon form. It had been a close call and one she vowed would not be repeated. She couldn't afford to miss a day in college, counting her lucky stars that it had been the summer break and that the slayer hadn't found his mark. She had been so intent on escaping that she didn't bother to fight back let alone see who her would-be slayer was. Orelle couldn't understand how the enmity between man and beast started. No matter how many times she googled dragons and dragonslayers, the hits were more about popular games and Wikipedia that didn't prove very informative. Meredith likely knew, but as a doyenne she was sworn to secrecy.

Orelle blew the steam away from her drink taking a gulp of the scalding liquid. She closed her eyes as it went down her throat, thawing her from inside out. She watched the tourists with interest, a faint smile appearing. There were families who had tiny tots in tow searching for a place to sit and take a break from their parental duties. She looked out the glass, her mug up to her lips when she stopped and sucked in a breath. Her stomach quivered with a gazillion excited butterflies.

Saxton.

He saw her and not even the glass between them could stop the heat in his eyes. When he entered the café striding purposefully towards her, Orelle's breathing hitched. Her heart thudded harder and her cheeks warmed. Saxton exuded suppressed strength and that cocky confidence letting her know that he was used to getting what he wanted. It was a far cry from how he looked when he served her food with a tea towel thrown over his shoulder and a chef's apron tied around his narrow waist. He had been boyishly handsome then.

Now he was all man. Raw, sexy, good enough to eat. His hair, darker when wet, and the stubble covering his jaw made him look like a total badass. The raindrops that stayed on his leather biker jacket slid down like water on duck feathers. His lopsided grin and the sensuality in his eyes directed only at her made her nipples pucker in response. But there was something else. Orelle caught a glimpse of a haunted look before it disappeared.

"Hi." His voice was soft almost tender but its effect on her was no different. Orelle just wanted to stand up and feel his body against hers once more.

"Hi." She could have kicked herself for sounding like an eager beaver. "Got caught in the rain?"

Saxton's mouth twitched, a dimple coming out.

"Something like that. Mind if I sit?"

"Mmm...not at all." Orelle took her lips off the rim of her mug. "Please. Want coffee?"

Saxton's eyes mirrored his amusement. "You buying?"

Her own mouth curved. She tilted her chin. "Unless chivalry is still alive and kicking, why not?"

He snorted softly. "I was just kidding. Want another of what you're having?"

Orelle leaned away from the table and set down her mug. She shook her head. "Thanks. I'm good." She watched him approach the counter, his denims hugging his ass, his muscular thighs...

Shit. Pussy's warming up for nothing.

Saxton returned with two puff pastries. "Thought you might want something with your coffee."

Orelle's lips curved to one side. "Remembered my love for eating, huh."

Saxton's mouth twitched. "Something like that."

Smiling her thanks, Orelle took one of the pastries and bit into it, humming in pleasure as the sweetness coated her mouth. She blushed furiously when Saxton watched her eating once again, focusing on her mouth. Warmth filled the pit of her belly before spreading through her. Saxton's eyes flared when she licked her fingers and Orelle couldn't stop the naughty act of popping her finger out of her mouth.

Remember who you are.

The warning felt like a cold bucket of water dousing her.

"What?" Orelle ignored the warning inside her head. "Yeah, I know. I eat like a slob."

Saxton's shoulders shook once, twice before his head moved in the negative. "You don't." He sipped his coffee, making a face. "Jesus we make better coffee!"

"Shhh!"

Thank God for the downpour practically drowning all conversation. They watched as the rains lashed at the glass walls. People who had been fine walking under the deluge ran inside the museum practically soaking wet despite their brollies and raincoats. The café's counter saw brisk business spike within minutes.

Saxton leaned forward. "You could have just gone to The Brew Bar. I would have made coffee for you."

"Uh...hello?" Orelle cocked a brow. "This was the closest shelter from the rain I could find?"

Saxton leaned back on his chair. When his knee touched hers under the table, Orelle's eyes widened in surprise at the spark of electricity that spiralled up her thigh to her core and spine. Saxton's gaze flashed and this time he didn't stop it from burning her.

"Why haven't you gone back to the bar?"

"No reason." She shrugged. "I'm spending the last few days of my freedom going where I want to go."

"Freedom?"

She laughed softly. "I teach at the local college.

Next time I have some time off will be when they break up for the next round of holidays."

"And classes start in a couple of weeks," he stated looking down at his coffee.

"Yes," she said, her eyes straying to the other uneaten pastry.

Saxton grinned, his sensual lips widening to show even teeth. He pushed the pastry toward her.

"Go on," he said, laughter in his voice. "I like watching."

"So you keep telling me." Orelle couldn't help it. Her eyes rolled and she giggled at the relaxed banter she was having with this sexy man. "Though I can't understand why."

"Why what?"

"Why you like watching me eat." She bit into the pastry and moaned. "This is so good."

A bit of the cream oozed from the pastry to coat the corner of her mouth. Saxton reached over and flicked it with his thumb. Orelle's breath suspended. Their eyes locked. They didn't speak. Orelle's heartbeat fluttered when Saxton offered his thumb for her to lick. Slowly, her tongue darted out first before she took his thumb into her mouth. Saxton's eyes darkened before his lids lowered watching how she pampered his digit. Blood thundered and rushed through her like white water rapids. Even her dragon opened one eye, snorted, swished its tail and went back to sleep as though its inattention was Orelle's signal to do whatever she wanted.

Her tongue swirled around Saxton's thumb and he shifted in his chair. Excitement traced a smile on her lips before she let go. Saxton rubbed his wet thumb against her bottom lip and the sensual play was felt all the way down to her soaking knickers, where a gentle throbbing started in her sex.

Saxton moved in closer, their face only inches apart, uncaring that there were people around them. Orelle searched his eyes, trying to find the man behind those dark haunted pools. Saxton's gaze slid down to her mouth once more. Orelle's breathing quickened when Saxton's mouth moved closer to hers. Her eyes fluttered, her body tensed as power from Saxton's touch coursed through her.

His lips brushed lightly over hers. Like before, they were firm and soft. But unlike before, the kiss was more exploratory, allowing her to control the pace. Orelle inhaled sharply, taking in his scent of man, musk and a woodsy cologne that had her leaning closer for more. Her dragon took notice, its belly inflating as it inhaled Saxton's scent that mimicked the earth it longed to revel in. Orelle tasted the bit of coffee he had, a dark roast. Much like the man. A sensual flame ignited inside her bringing a shaft of current to her nerve impulses, making her feel more alive than she had ever been. Her mind cautioned then begged not go give in but Orelle couldn't stop. Saxton's kiss, his mere presence was like a drug that she couldn't get enough of. When he gently sucked at her lower lip, she was gone.

"Sax...," she whispered when he let go to caress her jaw with his mouth.

CHAPTER EIGHT

What the fuck is happening?

Saxton ended the kiss. He saw his bemusement and desire mirrored in Orelle's eyes. Her lips tasted sweet – hints of vanilla, coffee, and cream. When he saw her mouth move over the pastry and the delicate way she started chewing...how could he get so turned with the way someone masticated their food? And when he couldn't stop himself from tasting from her lips once more, the scent he was getting addicted to became stronger. He needed to have her, feel her body under him, chart every bit of her skin with his tongue. He'd get her out of his system somehow and then he wouldn't be this overly infatuated schoolboy. He'd been through similar situations before and a good fuck was enough for him to move on. It was the only way he'd be able to clear his mind if he wanted to find the tranquillity only his dragon's death could give.

"Want to get out of here?" he rasped, not giving a rat's ass that his craving of her was evident in his tone.

"Where?" Orelle asked still dazed from his exploration. She was just as affected as he was. And her scent, bloody hell. He wanted to delve his tongue into her pussy and take everything she gave. The thought made his cock rock hard in his pants. His jacket wasn't long enough to hide his boner.

And he didn't give a bloody fuck.

His mouth twitched. "To get much better coffee."

Orelle laughed. That sound was sure as hell going to break his zipper now. She was driving him crazy with want.

Grabbing her hand before she could even put her coat on and take her purse hanging from the chair, Saxton led her out of the café.

And into another squall.

"Are you sure about this?" Orelle looked up uncertainly, water plopping on her face. She hurriedly donned her coat.

Saxton turned her to face him, cupped her face gently in his hands and kissed her. He basked in the air she expelled before his tongue breached her mouth to plunder its softness. And just like at the club, he felt her melt into him, holding on to his jacket tightly lest she fell. His arm moved lower to her waist, taking her with him while he continued to explore her mouth. She moaned when he ended the kiss.

"That answer enough?" She looked beautiful with her swollen lips and wonder filling her midnight blue eyes. He chuckled when all she did was nod, no sound coming out of her mouth. He sobered. "What have you done to me Orelle? I can't get enough of you."

He waited. Orelle's irises were almost

completely black.

"Then have me. Take me where you want me to go."

Saxton didn't have to be told twice. They charged into the squall. Coat and jacket were their only protection. Saxton didn't care. Behind him and more often, beside him, Orelle laughed with enjoyment. She raised her face to the rain and didn't care if people glanced at them with bemusement. Saxton just liked watching her and stopped walking when she stood at a standstill, turning her face to the sky once more, closing her eyes and allowing the heavens to soak her. Saxton's heart nearly burst inside his chest.

God, she is beautiful and she doesn't even realise it.

"Much as I like seeing you enjoying the rain, I'm beginning to freeze my butt off," he said. Water had started to coat the back of his shirt and his muscles tightened against the elements.

Orelle giggled and extended her hand. Her features softened. "Let's go."

Saxton couldn't stop his grin and the elation that increased inside his chest. He couldn't remember a time when he had enjoyed being with a woman who enjoyed simple things like walking in the rain. Most of the time, it was a woman who couldn't wait to get into his pants and take his cock into her mouth. Orelle wasn't a woman who screeched at the first drops of rain whining about her make-up and hair or clothes. Confidence oozed from her, a kind of devil-may-care-just-live-for-the-day attitude. That turned him on. All he could think of now was getting Orelle out of her wet clothes and into his bed.

They arrived at the back door of The Brew Bar, both exhaling within the warm confines once the door closed behind them. The muffled sounds of pots and pans clanging over hobs and shouted orders reached their ears from the kitchen just to their left. Its stark white fluorescent light streamed through the door's porthole and into the softly lit corridor where they stood. To the right of the corridor was a flight of stairs and Saxton led the way to the third floor, the wood creaking under the strain of their thudding shoes. Once they reached the landing, he led the way through a wider corridor and stopped in front of a third wooden door. He preceded Orelle inside and watched as she looked around the self-contained bachelor pad each of the slayers had above The Brew Bar.

"There's a clean bathrobe in the closet over there," he pointed to an armoire in the corner by the window as he closed the door.

Orelle moved into the middle of the room, her flat leather ankle boots making soft sounds on the floor.

He pointed to another door on the opposite corner. "Bathroom's in there. I'll get us something to drink. Be right back."

She turned in place taking in the wooden sleigh bed with a single side table, the matching chest of drawers, the wooden beams and mullioned windows protecting them from the rain that continued to slash against the glass, before her eyes met his.

"Can the drinks wait?" Her soft voice floated towards him, her need barely suppressed.

In two strides Saxton was in front of her, his own hunger spilling out of him and into her mouth as their lips locked. Heated breaths joined the slick sounds of jackets falling to the floor and wet clothes being shed. A satisfied growl rose up Saxton's throat when he finally felt Orelle's skin against his. His hands ran down her damp body moving to squeeze her ass, flushing her close so that his hard throbbing cock pulsed against her belly. She gasped and Saxton forged into her mouth. Holy heaven, he nearly trembled. How the fuck could he be so affected by Orelle that her every touch and most of all the scent she emitted made him want to live longer? It almost made him rethink his quest to vanquish his dragon and live a life without a soul. With Orelle, he felt he already had one.

Blood roared in his ears at her sighs and the tiny moans that pumped more blood into his already hard dick. Her tongue slid against his, tangling in an erotic play with seductive ease. She licked and sucked on his lips sending jolts of lust down his aching cock and tightening balls. Her arms that encircled his neck now travelled down his shoulders, his skin flexing when her fingers trailed down his chest. He groaned putting open kisses against her neck when she rubbed his nipples to hard points. Everywhere Orelle touched was like a lick of flame jumpstarting him. With one flick of his fingers against her back, he unhooked her bra. His mouth kissed her shoulder from where the strap fell from. With one arm under her knees, Saxton carried Orelle to the bed, his knee dipping against the mattress. But he didn't let her go. Bracing her back with his arm, he slowly arched her as he leaned forward to take a rosy hardened peak into his mouth. Her honeyed sweetness filled his taste buds and his cock twitched at the sounds coming out from her lips. Damn, his balls were heavy and he didn't want to climax unless he was inside Orelle.

"Saxton..." she whispered.

He couldn't wait any longer. A hunger to have a woman like no other filled him. He lay her down on the bed, his mouth kissing as much flesh as he could before his need to taste her consumed him. Her stomach dipped with his every caress, his every kiss. His hand lowered shaping her hip before his fingers moved to her centre. Orelle spread her legs. Saxton rose up once more to kiss her before removing her knickers to play with her slit.

"Yes..." Orelle's hips bucked against his fingers as he explored her wetness, her hands cupping his face as her tongue flicked against his mouth, her breath coming out fast.

"Oh baby you're so tight. Your pussy's sucking my finger so good. I want it to suck my tongue and cock too." He groaned against her ear before running his mouth against the column of her throat. "Tell me to stop, Orelle. I won't be able to if you don't."

"No," she panted. "Why would I do that if I want

you to fuck me?"

* * *

Orelle was so wet her lust trickled down the crack of her ass. She couldn't help herself from searching for his shaft with her hand wanting its head against her opening. Saxton hissed when she found his hot shaft and closed her hand around it, pumping him gently, pre-cum dripping against her fingers.

"Ahh fuck it, Orelle."

Saxton rose so suddenly, Orelle looked at him in a daze. None to gently, she squealed when he left the bed and dragged her to the edge. He knelt on the floor as he spread her legs wide. Lust and anticipation made her heart race as she looked down at him, her face heating up at the raw hunger on his face.

"So pink, bare and wet for me," Saxton said almost reverently. "So beautiful."

Orelle shuddered when his fingers grazed her gently and rubbed her clit with his thumb. Saxton looked up, his eyes dark with his intent. No words were spoken. Only gazes locked before he bent down and swiped her cleft with this tongue. Orelle gasped and soon closed her eyes as his tongue found her sweet spot. Not even when Saxton gripped her thighs, widening her for his mouth did she open them, caught up in the sensations that zinged all over her body. She rolled her hips while his mouth devoured her pussy. She was caught in a vortex of ecstasy that had her moaning, whimpering, and clutching the sheets as waves of pleasure coursed through her.

"Yes…" Oh Lord, she trembled as Saxton flicked his tongue against her clit in fast intervals before flattening it.

"You taste so good." The sweet sounds Saxton's mouth made caused her to bite her bottom lip in sheer bliss. Her hands went to his head to run her fingers through his thick wet mane. She cried out softly when he closed his lips over her bundle of nerves while a finger then two entered her, coaxing her lust to spiral higher.

"Oh shit, oh shit…" she whimpered, her head dipping further on the bed. She was so close but when she was about to come, Saxton would slow down. "Bloody hell, Saxton don't tease me anymore!"

His chuckled rumbled against her adding to the pleasure building inside her. He touched her, seared her, brought her a little bit closer but not quite towards completion. He opened his mouth and inserted his tongue inside her hole, taking her everywhere ecstasy hid. Her hips bucked against his mouth both in surprise and hunger. She craved for him to touch her in places she didn't realise were in her. Places that allowed her to spiral upwards, burning her with a brighter fire than her dragon inside her ever could. When she covered his hands with her own, raising them to her chest, Orelle rocked against his mouth while they both squeezed her breasts, pinching her hardened nubs. She raised her head and their gazes met across her grinding hips and Saxton's voracious mouth. She was getting close to where Saxton wanted her to be. Her breathing stuttered in her throat and her thighs trembled.

"Sax…"

"Hold your legs and spread them wider for me, Orelle," he commanded in a voice she didn't recognize but obeyed. He moved his fingers inside her, flicking them faster and faster as he sucked on her clit. Orelle could no longer contain the pressure in the pit of her belly. Her body sizzled and a thunderous wave of ecstasy rolled over her. She screamed as she drowned in the whirlpool of lust Saxton created for her. Her climax was so intense that she literally saw stars in front of her eyes. She felt suspended in the rafters of pleasure before it let her go, her cries softening as she came back down, boneless and spent. Outside it rained harder, keeping them isolated from the rest of the world.

With a swipe of his tongue and a chaste kiss on her pampered pussy, Saxton rose, rewarding her with his body over hers. When he kissed her, Orelle chased after his teasing mouth, her neck straining upwards begging for him to deepen the kiss he teasingly denied her. When his tongue darted out, Orelle captured and sucked it, tasting herself. Then he ended the intimacy of their mouths. His hooded eyes still made her heat up with desire still mirrored in them. His gaze caressed her face while he made himself comfortable between her thighs. Orelle's hands roamed his back and shoulders as her feet glided up and down the back of his legs. Smooth skin with corded strength underneath quivered under her touch.

"What have you done to me Orelle?" he whispered for the hundredth time. His voice was almost puzzled, disbelieving. Orelle heard the sadness underlying Saxton's words as though there was something waiting for him on the other end of a green mile he had to traverse.

She traced her finger over his bottom lip. Saxton grinned and playfully nipped at it. She could have also asked the same thing. Apart from the feelings he evoked in her, Saxton made her wish she was a normal person with normal cares. Not someone who could shift into a huge flying reptile complete with claws and horns that could gore five people at a time. He made her wish for a small house outside the city, a place where they could stay and explore each other until there was nothing left to explore before doing it all over again. She longed for more moments with Saxton to get to know the man underneath that taut muscled body that brought her so much pleasure. For the first time in her life, Orelle was really afraid. Women of her kind left men, but she couldn't see herself leaving Saxton. If that was the case, how could she tell him what she really was?

Yet, all 'what if' thoughts melted into the 'here and now' when all she could think of was Saxton hovering over her, watching and caressing her face with his gaze as he nudged himself inside her.

"Oh lord, you're thick," she gasped out a laugh as she moved her hips to accommodate him. The pinch of pain at the way Saxton stretched her brought her even more pleasure. She looked into his eyes before she moaned when he rubbed his cock against her clit before edging back to her opening.

Saxton didn't speak. He just watched her as he bucked his hips slowly, entering and then withdrawing. Each gentle thrust sending pleasurable impulses up her spine and to the nerves around her pussy. Orelle raised her own hips in welcome. No words would ever describe what passed between them. It was beyond lust, beyond seduction, beyond sex in just a short space of time. Saxton was taking a part of her with him and she felt its pull with every fibre of her being. Something wanted to dislodge itself from around that beating muscle inside her chest. Saxton continued to push in...deeper and the flaking of that unfamiliar coating around her heart intensified. Uncomfortable. Not painful.

It was bittersweet.

When Saxton withdrew and thrust in once again to the hilt, Orelle closed her eyes, a sigh escaping her lips as bliss filled her. Saxton lowered his forehead to hers, his eyes closed, his jaw clenched.

"Ahh...Orelle." His musk surrounded her. "So fucking tight." He withdrew and leaned up before he plunged deep inside her. Her pussy muscles clamped around him as desire exploded inside her causing her to whimper. Saxton braced himself on his arms, his knees digging a hold on the mattress. Orelle locked her legs around his back, urging him to take her.

"Mine," Saxton's dark eyes were filled with

intensity. He thrust hard, his balls slapping against her. Orelle gasped and whimpered in pleasure. She held on to him afraid that she might fall into some chasm she'd never get out from. "You're mine, Orelle. Only mine."

Saxton commanded the rhythm, his thrusts quickening and feeding Orelle's hunger, easing the ache inside her. He leaned to one side, gripping her ass when she bowed at the ecstasy licking at her. He pinned her where he wanted her, feeding his cock into her and she took him in willingly, her sex becoming a rock bed of pleasure that sent sparks flying all over her body. She was putty in his hands. Exquisite pressure began to build once more, adding fuel to the fire. The bed creaked, the headboard slamming against the wall as the rain lashed against the windows and drowning their noise. Bodies melded, joined in a glorious desire that swirled around them locking them inside their own cocoon as they left the world behind. Orelle's release caught her unawares and she screamed for the second time. Her pussy muscles clamped and throbbed around Saxton's cock. With a guttural groan Saxton spilled himself into her, thrusting twice more before he gently fell on her. His seed warmed her womb and intense emotion Orelle could not describe made her want to cry. She felt his rapid beating heart against her own fluttering one, their bodies coated in a sheen of sweat. After a while, Saxton moved about to ease himself to the side.

"No. Please…stay," she whispered.

His breath fanned her face when he chuckled. "I'm too heavy."

Orelle kept him between her legs. She caressed his sweaty face before kissing him.

"Stay."

CHAPTER NINE

Saxton let Orelle sleep on the rumpled sheets. After taking her once more until tears slid down the sides of her face Saxton thought he wouldn't be able to get out of bed for the next several hours. Orelle's fresh meadows and wild flowers scent filled the room mixed with the smell of their lovemaking. Saxton wouldn't have had it any other way. They hadn't used protection too intent on getting at each other to fuck like rabbits and think of the consequences later. But the thought that Orelle might carry his child brought a fuzzy warmth to his gut. To see her grow with a bun in the oven brought his protective instinct out.

Whoa!

Fuck, he was so screwed. He dry rubbed his face. He'd talk to her once she woke from her fuck-me-til-kingdom-come induced sleep.

He had watched her. The way she breathed, the way her lips softly parted to let air into her lungs. The half-moon sweep of her lashes over her closed eyelids. The flush of sex on her skin.

Damn, his cock was asking for another round so he staggered out of the bed to put on a new pair of dark jeans, a fresh shirt and shoes and quietly left the room to get the drinks he was supposed to have gotten earlier. But first, he had to get her clothes into the wash. He grinned. It was going to take longer to get her clothes dry.

When he arrived at the bar, the tables were heaving with lunch patrons with a queue still waiting by the bar's entrance. The foyer was crowded with waiting diners with dripping umbrellas and windbreakers. It was a mixture of office workers and families making the most of the last few days of the holidays before the house-school-house run dominated their lives once more.

The restaurant was full. Bar staff went in and out of the kitchen with trays laden with food while their bartender was kept busy getting the drink orders ready before another member of the staff whisked the drinks tray away. The volume of conversation nearly drowned the piped in music.

Sabine was busy getting the orders of those lining the counter waiting for their turn, helped by the rest of the bar staff they hired - uni students wanting to earn extra money. Saxton inched his way behind the counter to get two squat glasses and filled them with two fingers of single malt each. He and Sabine stood side by side, her movements jerky as she slid her card on the side of the cash register and tapping the orders on to the monitor. Saxton darted a glance her way.

"Listen –"

"Forget it," Sabine muttered. She closed the till turning around with a practised smile to hand over the change to a customer. She briefly turned to

Saxton, hand on her hip. "Just one of those days."

Sabine's more genuine smile told Saxton that everything was all right between them. No one could fault her dedication to them, collectively known as the Pinehaven slayers. She knew who they were and kept their secrets probably better than the Bank of England's vault. She was also a formidable opponent when they sparred during the rare times they invited her to do so. No one knew where she came from but her gratitude was as boundless as her sassy attitude that hid a tragedy Sabine refused to speak of. She was a slayer without a family to call her own so the men decided to take her into their care.

Fences mended, Saxton left the noisy bar, eager to return to Orelle until Theo met him along the corridor.

"Sax, a word."

"I'm busy. Can't it wait?"

Theo's eyes glimmered with amusement. "Have you finished the books?"

"No," he said. It reminded him of why he stormed out of the bar in the first place. "It's nearly done. I'll finish it later."

"Why is it taking long? You normally finish them in record time."

Saxton looked down at the floor. "Ty arrived. I needed air."

Theo's mocking grin disappeared. He snorted with repugnance. "What did he want?"

"Nothing I couldn't handle. Told him to fuck off."

"Good for you." Theo clapped Saxton's shoulder. He nudged his head towards the stairs. "Whoever it is you have upstairs must be wondering whether you found someone else if you've been here downstairs this long."

"Jackass."

Theo grinned and winked. "Thank you."

Saxton took the steps two at a time. What Theo said surprisingly hit a nerve. Find someone else? He just wanted Orelle.

Orelle was just stirring when he returned to the room. Her hair dishevelled, she had the I've-just-been-fucked-really-good look. Saxton grinned.

I did that.

"Hey." She smiled at him. She took the proffered drink. "Thanks."

Saxton's brow rose. "Thought you'd want something to drink, but I didn't peg you for a scotch drinker."

"I'm not." Orelle belatedly grimaced. She swallowed slowly. "But it was cold. Ugh, how can anyone stomach this taste?"

"Acquired taste." He raised his glass to her before taking a huge sip. The fire running down his throat felt good. He placed his glass on the side table. "Cold, huh? I thought I more than warmed you up."

She sat up as she nearly sputtered. A blush bloomed on her cheeks. "Yes, you did."

Saxton eased himself to lean against the headboard. He opened his arm and felt his world turn upside down at her smile before she sidled to his side, taking the light blanket with her. His mouth quirked at her contented sigh. He took a sip from his drink while he ran his fingers over her arm.

"We need to talk."

Orelle stiffened slightly. She sat up gingerly, holding the sheet against her chest. Her face was puzzled. "Talk about what?"

"I didn't use a condom."

She stared at him blankly before her eyes twinkled softly.

"What?" It was his turn to look bemused.

"No guy has talked to me about not using protection."

"I'm clean, believe me."

"Good to know," she mocked. "And thank you. I'm on the pill so no harm done." She gave him an assessing look. "You're different."

Saxton looked down at his drink. "How so?"

"You shag a woman yet care to tell her you weren't careful."

"And that's different because?"

"Men leave it all up to the woman to sort things out."

"Yeah well," Saxton put both their glasses down on the bedside table. "We're assholes that way. Besides, you can't live without us."

"Really?" Orelle's brows rose so high. "Guess you've never heard of B.O.B."

Saxton laughed, his shoulders shaking. "That thing doesn't hold a candle to us flesh and blood."

"You're being a dick."

"No. I'm saying you've got the real thing so you don't need it."

"And I'm saying that we can live without you."

"Ouch." He placed his hand over his chest. "You wound me."

And it did sting. That was a first. To think that Orelle could live without him caught him off guard, bringing pain in his chest that made it almost difficult to breathe.

Orelle puffed out a laugh. She pulled away, taking the sheet with her. Saxton felt the empty coldness where she left his side.

"Where are you going?"

"Home."

"Really? And are you planning on walking out of here buck naked?"

* * *

Orelle stopped.

Shit.

The coolness of the room skittered over her naked back and buttocks exposed and framed by the sheets. She felt the bed dip when Saxton crawled and stayed behind her. She shivered as his heat warmed her back through his shirt. She clutched the sheet tighter to her chest despite part of her mind saying 'let go!'. She sat straighter, startled the moment Saxton's finger tranced her spine. Goose bumps followed in its wake and her nipples puckered once more.

"Sax, I really need to go," she said her voice,

husky. She closed her eyes when she felt Saxton's warm breath against her shoulder before he nipped at it. Orelle craned her neck to the side to give him better access to the column of her throat, and oh Lord....He traced the shell of her ear with his tongue. She reached up, her fingers ploughing through his dark hair before turning to give Saxton a languid kiss. Saxton's hands caressed her waist, the heat warming her before they travelled up to play with her breasts.

"Saxton...please..."

"Please what?" His deep voice made her damp once more. "Please suck your tits?"

Orelle groaned.

"No?" His tone was teasing. "How about I play with your pussy?"

"Sax..." Orelle didn't recognize her voice and she didn't care. She was aching inside.

His deep rumble brought a shiver of desire down her spine just has Saxton's hand lowered to nudge her legs apart and dipped into her folds. Purring, Orelle leaned back against Saxton's chest as she gave in to his strumming like how a lover strummed a guitar. The sheet fell away from her and Orelle had to grip the bed as she was tossed once more in a sea of desire. Her hips bucked when Saxton's fingers delved inside her sex, coaxing out more of her silky wetness.

"Fuck, Orelle. You're driving me insane," Saxton growled.

"Can't Sabine lend me some clothes?" she asked, trying to hold on to a semblance of sanity before she was catapulted over the stratosphere. She shuddered when he nipped at her shoulder.

"She could," he replied while he continued to slide his fingers in and out of her. "But if you dressed, you'll be depriving me of playing with your pussy. And this," Orelle gasped when he tapped her clit gently. "Belongs to me, Orelle. No one will ever have your sweet pussy but me."

Orelle gripped his wrist with a cry the moment he plunged three fingers inside her. Oh God, the feeling was exquisitely tight and so good. She felt stretched and sore in the most delicious of ways. The way he finger fucked her made her beg for more.

"That's it baby." Saxton's voice was hoarse. "I like seeing you come undone. Can you feel that, Orelle? I want my hand to be wet with your pussy's cream. That's it, hold my wrist and let's both finger fuck you."

Orelle didn't care anymore. Saxton's dirty talk was driving her insane with lust. She needed her release so she did what she was told. She fucked herself with Saxton's hand.

And she came.

But there was no scream that shattered the four walls of the room.

Saxton had covered her mouth with his.

And claimed her release for himself.

Orelle was completely sated. She vaguely felt herself being gently moved to the middle of the bed. She wiggled against Saxton's clothed body, putting a thigh over his groin. Saxton grunted and faced her.

"You're right," she said, her eyes still closed and

waiting for her breathing to normalize.

Saxton kissed the top of her head.

"About what?" His voice rumbled like a river of dark chocolate under her ear.

"About B.O.B. You're sooo much better than B.O.B."

The last thing Orelle heard was Saxton's bark of laughter before she was pulled under towards a blissful sleep once more.

CHAPTER TEN

There was still a big smile on Orelle's face when she parked her car in Havenshade's courtyard. She couldn't stop the grin even if she tried. With Saxton, she no longer knew what day it was. First she agreed to stay until her clothes were washed and dried. Then Saxton convinced her to stay longer until she firmly said she had to go. She didn't give him her number. He didn't give his either though she knew where he worked and lived half of the time. While disappointing, it was better that way. This was just one long tryst where they both got what they wanted out of it. End of story.

Switching the engine off, she looked up, the smile freezing before dying on her face.

Something is wrong.

Night had fallen by the time she arrived in the lair, but that wasn't what started alarm bells ringing.

Havenshade was pitch dark.

Orelle sprinted to the entrance.

"Ara?"

Orelle closed the door behind her, her eyes easily adjusting to the dark. It wasn't like Ara to be quiet. Even when she was in the small room at the end of the house where she concocted her potions for dragon wounds like what had happened to Orelle, music constantly blared through the gap underneath the closed door. What human hearing picked up as normal was loud for them.

At the moment, Orelle couldn't even hear soft.

Leaving her keys and purse on the small foyer table, Orelle ran up the stairs.

"Ara!" Orelle called once more before reaching Ara's bedroom door. "Ar...shit!" she rushed into the room. What she saw made her blood turn to ice. Ara was on the floor, her breathing shallow, her eyes were fever bright and had taken on the vertical pupils of her dragon.

"Orelle." She wheezed. Her voice was gravelly almost masculine and malevolent, but Orelle knew it was the transitioning. Ara was moulting for the first time. Green, gold, and brown patched her skin like some body paint quilt work. Her human flesh was being taken over by her dragon.

"We need to get you out of here," Orelle said gently. "To the woods." She made to stand but Ara gripped her arm that couldn't have easily crushed her bones. Orelle ground her teeth to stop the cry of pain from Ara's death grip. She could feel Ara's restraint in her hold, could sense Ara now knew what she was now capable of.

"Water...I need...water. Remember?"

Orelle's heart tumbled in dismay. Ara wasn't talking about a drink of water or a simple shower.

How could she have forgotten? Ara's element was water. Problem was, they had to drive a distance to get to a body of water that was big enough for Ara to allow her dragon its first free rein. To the reservoirs.

"I'll get you to water but you need to let me go first." Orelle spoke softly not anymore just to Ara but to the dragon as well. She made her own dragon's heart beat and synch with Ara's dragon. She soothed it, calmed it until she could hear Ara's dragon inside her head. It was backing down.

When the women were born with their dragons, the beasts didn't automatically show themselves until they were good and ready. For a time they could live in relative peace, have uncomplicated relationships and enjoy what the mortal world had to offer. The dragon's appearance was similar to a coming of age or rite of passage.

After a hundred years, it was Ara's turn.

"Where are you going?" Her voice rasped. Apprehension tingled down Orelle's spine at the dragon's voice.

"I need to take your duvet and soak it in water," Orelle explained then added quickly. "Until I get you to the reservoirs."

Ara immediately let go of Orelle's arm, her hand flopping down on the wooden floor with a thud. Orelle rushed to the bathroom, turning the tap to full until the duvet was completely soaked. It left a water trail across the floor and a puddle framing Ara's body.

Orelle carefully wrapped Ara, who kept hissing, as she rolled into the wet fabric. Pulling from her own dragon's strength, she carried a thickly wrapped

Ara in her arms as water soaked her clothes once more.

"Orelle..." How could a pitiful cry coated in a masculine voice make her heart crack a little? Simple. Orelle knew the pain and fear of the unknown that Ara was going through now. But her dragon sister was strong. Once Ara finally moulted, she'd be all the better for it.

Provided they reached the reservoirs fast.

Ladybower reservoir was located in the Upper Derwent Valley in Derbyshire. From Snake Road, the reservoir looked serpentine, a slithering giant that glittered under the pale moonlight. There were no lights in this part of the moors. The only navigational guides drivers had were the speed limit and road signs telling them whether a chicane was up ahead, the reflectorized guides in the middle of the road or the arrows telling them they were about to round a bend. This was no place for a drunk to speed through the night fantasizing that he had just joined the Paris – Dakkar race. Only parts of Snake Pass had wired fences and dry walls. Poor brake reflexes could do three things: first, propel a car into a ravine, hurl it against hapless trees, or second, wait until the trunks gave way allowing the vehicle to plunge into the cold waters of the reservoir. No one would be able to hear any cries for help. The last one was the more merciful one: they already had an appointment with their maker prior to plunging to their mortal death.

It didn't take long for Orelle and Ara to reach the

reservoir. Snake Road was practically deserted as Orelle gunned the accelerator, her sharp eyes anticipating twists and turns of the pass. The nearest well of civilization from Havenshade was Glossop and at ten in the evening it looked deserted.

"Almost there." She took a quick glance at the rearview mirror. Her hands gripped the steering wheel so hard her knuckles showed white.

Ara's growing tail made a thud against the back of the driver's seat and nearly threw Orelle against the steering wheel. She hissed at the pain just by the side of her spine when one of Ara's tail horns pierced her skin. Her blood gushed and soaked the back of her shirt. It wasn't deep and it would heal eventually, but it sure as hell was going to leave a nasty bruise. Thank God for leather seats. She could easily wipe her blood off it later.

Orelle came to a grinding stop inside the car park inching as close as she could get to the reservoir. It was dark everywhere allowing them the cover they needed. A slight breeze rippled through the trees cordoning off the parking lot. Even the breeze kissed the surface of the water that lapped gently against the banks. Taking Ara out of the car, Orelle walked as fast as she could to the reservoir's edge. The water had receded.

Shit.

Orelle staved off the panic threatening to overwhelm her at hearing Ara wheezing and her breathing becoming shallow. Her arms strained from

Ara's increasing weight. Her sister dragon was getting heavier now that she had allowed her foundling to take over.

Orelle laid Ara down the sandy bank and peeled the damp blanket away. She gasped at Ara's mid transformation. Her legs were already spread apart to accommodate her elongating torso and a tail that stretched out once it was out of the duvet. Her hair was mottled and huge gill like protrusions peeked out of the tangled mass beside her face and over her head. Her face was elongated, her snout puffing out sulphuric smoke and her teeth had started to lengthen and filling her mouth.

"Ara, can you hear me?" Orelle asked softly, her own dragon's heart soothing Ara's scared one. "It will be all right. Take all the time you need in the water, okay?"

Her reptilian eyes blinked. She nodded.

Orelle blew out a relieved breath. "I'm going to roll you to the water's edge then you're on your own. Understand?"

"Get...me...to...the water...Orelle."

Pain lanced through Orelle at the sound of Ara's plaintive whimpers. Pleading and afraid, yet resolute. Nodding, Orelle rolled Ara's body across the few feet to the water's edge, the wetness lapping at her shoes just as she stepped back. And waited.

In the dark, Orelle saw her dragon sister struggle. Her snout was at the water's edge. Her laboured breathing slowly eased as she took in the scent of her element. Ara used the underside of her snout and belly to propel herself forward, her body starting to undulate just as it had been created to do since the beginning of time. Her hands and feet, now claws sank into the moist earth as she moved forward. Then she was gone, sinking into the depths until her dragon was ready to surface. Orelle sank down on the damp bank, the wetness seeping into the seat of her denims but she didn't care. She was just incredibly relieved that she had arrived in Havenshade in time. She drew a breath and exhaled as she lay down on the drier part of the bank.

She couldn't stop berating herself. If she hadn't been with Saxton, she wouldn't be rushing through roads and teasing the speed limits. There would have been plenty of time to prepare for Ara's first moulting. Then again, no one knew when the dragons decided to make their debut. Not even their human hosts.

After Ara's entry into the water, the surface of Ladybower became glasslike once more, the ripples having exhausted itself against the banks on both sides of the reservoir. It was the best place for her sister dragon to be in.

Orelle scanned the darkness around her, quickly identifying the copse of trees that emitted the faint scent of pine that always soothed her. They stood tall and proud even if their roots clawed at the slopes that seemed to roll on to forever. Tall majestic beings that held the secrets of the ages in the rings within their trunks.

Looking up at the stars Orelle relaxed and her thoughts returned to Saxton. Her body still hummed, a gentle charge of electricity sizzling underneath her skin. Even her dragon felt replete satisfied, curling its golden tail around itself in repose. The electrical charge caused her core to twitch, her sex throbbing in remembrance of the way Saxton took her. She covered her eyes with her arm and shook her head. Like that would dispel the guilt gnawing at her.

"What the hell have I gotten into?" she muttered for the hundredth time.

Saxton seemed to have successfully planted himself in her mind. None of the men she had had relationships with had been able to do so. The gently wind that passed over the surface of the water caressed her skin just like Saxton's lips. Her nipples puckered inside her bra, reliving the way he sucked and licked at them. She sighed when she thought of his incredible tongue on her sex. She thought that after she had slaked her sexual thirst, she'd forget him and move on. One torrid fuck session should have done the trick then she'd leave. Thing was, the thought of Saxton forgetting her left a sour taste in her mouth but Orelle chalked it up to envy at the next woman who'd be the recipient of his body. She just didn't expect it to churn her gut.

"Shit," she muttered. The best way to let go of this suddenly ingrained infatuation was to make sure she didn't bump into him in town. She'd avoid The

Brew Bar despite Saxton saying to drop by. A temptation she couldn't do without but a resolution she had to abide by. Thank God for small favours that Saxton didn't know where she lived in the city. It still remained her fortress of solitude.

But her body still thrummed with the remnants of her afternoon delight. Her sex started to throb as though her pulse decided to take a holiday to the south of her waist. A cool breeze rustled the trees and over her and all Orelle could think of was Saxton's warm breath against her neck while she was on top of him, holding her tightly against him as he thrust into her in ever increasing strokes that were quick and hard until she combusted with another scream Saxton took into himself before he followed her. His cock remained hard even after he was spent and kept moving inside her, the friction against her sex easily hyping her up for another of several rounds of fucktastic lust before she closed her eyes in exhaustion.

Her hand caressed her body out involuntarily, unbuttoning her jeans and moving into her soaked cleft. Orelle didn't believe she'd get caught but the possibility brought a dangerous kind of excitement slithering down her spine. Her fingers tried to mimic Saxton's tongue and fingers, sliding between her slick folds and finding her bundle of nerves. Her eyes closed on a gasp and a moan rose up her throat as her sex thickened with blood and sucked her fingers the way it sucked Saxton's mouth. She felt the pressure all too soon, her thoughts so vivid imagining Saxton smiling down at her while he fucked her. Her back bowed from the rocky ground as her orgasm ripped through her on a released breath.

"Saxton…"

CHAPTER ELEVEN

Pinehaven sat on a hill overlooking the moors where cloud fog and strong winds kept it away from prying eyes. A private road wended discreetly away from the main mountain road. It had a spectacular view of the land around it – from the Alport Castles in the west to the Hope Valley reservoirs in the east. To anyone passing by, Pinehaven looked like a manor and farm in the middle of nowhere. It had to be if the dragonslayers wanted their defence system to be hiding in plain sight. Pinehaven's defence centre against any dragon incursion was located under the farmhouse where the control systems of the low frequency seismic detector, a modified electronic scanning array that used low frequency radar, and chemical sensors were located. The sensors which detected the metabolites of a dragon's breath were part of the windmill vanes above ground which also brought energy into the farmhouse.

The minute Saxton entered the house with Braden, he heard Orelle's voice and smelled her scent around him.

"Saxton…"

His mouth twitched unable to stop his grin. Damn his imagination for thinking her to be close by.

"Looks like someone's got the cream." Braden

looked at him amused. "Literally."

Saxton glowered at Braden who raised his palms. "Chill out man! It's not like I don't diss all the women you slayers fuck."

"I've always known you had a foul mouth." Saxton pointed at him in irritation.

"And it's not okay to diss Orelle because?"

"Because she's different." Saxton scowled at the knowing look on Braden's face.

"Right, okay. Cool." Braden retreated, rolling his eyes.

Saxton strode across the huge airy living room with comfortable leather couches surrounding a low coffee table. The overhead wood beams sported recessed lights that glowed over the area. He moved to the opposite wall to open the huge French doors leading to the patio. He inhaled long and deep, Orelle's scent never leaving him, before he let his breath out slowly puffing in the frigid air.

He couldn't get enough her, even after they had both tired out, he still wanted more. Her sweet taste lingered on his tongue. Her featherlike touch ghosted over his skin and his cock twitched at the remembrance of her mouth around him.

Saxton tucked his hands into his jeans. Bloody hell, Orelle was still in his thoughts an hour after she'd left his bed. That was a first.

"Fuck." Air whooshed out of his nostrils. In the distance, he saw the waters of the reservoir glitter through the fog's haze. He took the binoculars from the table just inside the French doors and started checking the perimetre. He trained the binoculars on the reservoir that looked like a concrete snake in stasis expecting it be smooth. He frowned before looking through the lenses once more. The waters were slightly choppy. There were no storms in the area. The moon was high in the sky and the winds in his part of the vale hardly caused a massive ripple on the water's surface.

"Heracles," he called to Braden.

"Apollo," Braden rushed up the steps from the basement, his eyes wild. "Dragons. I can smell it all the way from here."

Saxton nodded then stilled. Orelle's scent wafted with the breeze coming through. Shit, he was hallucinating.

"Apollo!" Braden snapped using Saxton's slayer name.

Saxton walked to the door behind one of the couches. Punching in a combination, the door opened to show a well-lit armoury of battle axes, lances, and swords on one side and the dragonslayer's body armour made of ancient dragon hide on the other. Taking out his battle axes, Saxton secured it behind his back just as Braden took out one of the spears. They couldn't kill the dragon when they found it especially if it wasn't their Omega.

There wasn't anything in the playbook that said they couldn't injure it.

Saxton took the wheel of the DS5 hybrid driving at breakneck speed through another road from the farmhouse to the east. Dragons were fast. Once they realized that a slayer was nearby, they would disappear and hide under the rock they crawled out from. The frustrating thing was that when dragons took human form the slayers couldn't sniff them out. Maiming them on an exposed part of their body would ensure that they could be spotted in the crowd.

Which was a dumb solution as far as Saxton was concerned. But back in the day when there had been fewer people on earth, it had been sound. The rules hadn't been changed ever since.

His face was stony. Orelle's smell was still strong around him. Even the wind had her scent the closer they got to the reservoir. *Fuck.* He couldn't lose focus, couldn't get derailed by his wayward hunger for a woman he met at a club. A woman who made him believe there was life beyond killing his dragon. Orelle could even be that woman to replace his soul.

She was that perfect.

"Over there! Step on it!"

Saxton ground his teeth, his knuckles white against the steering wheel that threatened to bolt out of his grip. Braden was an asshole probably just like his namesake. The vehicle jumped and bumped over the rutted road. Loose stones pinged and thwacked the chassis underneath. Saxton shifted gears, the car changing to all terrain before they came to an abrupt stop that nearly ejected them from their seats. End of the road.

They now had to traverse on foot.

* * *

Orelle immediately sat up at the violent splash a few metres away from her. She stood straightening her shirt and jeans and grabbed the sodden duvet before rushing to Ara. The hem of her jeans and shoes took in water when she ran to the water's edge, sending ripples across the liquid surface.

"Orelle," Ara gasped, shivering and naked. Exhaustion and fear filled her face dripping with water. "Slayers!"

Orelle hissed, her eyes narrowing at the distance. In her human form, she was unable to pick out the slayers scent. Ara would, having just transformed.

"How far?" Orelle's voice was cold. It wasn't because Ara's foundling decided to moult that day. Her sister was weak from her first foray even though the water had satisfied her beast.

"They're nearing." Ara sighed, her lids drooping. "I'm so sleepy."

"I know, sweetie. We'll get you to bed but we have to get to the car first. Your bed will be warm and cozy." Orelle threw the duvet around Ara's naked shoulders and hauled her in a fireman's carry rushing as fast as she could to the car. Shit, there was blood on the bank where she lay. She couldn't do anything about that now and only hoped that the water rose again to remove it.

She gingerly placed an already sleeping Ara on the backseat. Orelle closed the door before taking the driver's seat without securing her seatbelt. Starting the engine, she stomped hard on the accelerator and reversed with her car's tires screeching against the asphalt just as she saw the slayers chasing them on foot. Their weapons gleamed in the light. Her heart jumped to her throat and an involuntary whimper escaped her as her hold on her self-control slipped. She mis-shifted and the car nearly lost power.

"No, no, no," she screamed. "Get a grip, Orelle! You're better than this!"

Finally the clutch engaged. The moment Orelle put pedal to the metal, the car zoomed away. She looked at her rearview mirror. A slayer with a long spear pulled back in a motion to throw his weapon at them. His companion grabbed his arm, stalling him.

The blood drained from her face and she nearly swerved again into a ditch. Bile rose up her throat and threatened to spill any minute. Pulling on whatever resolved she had left, Orelle kept her eyes on the road taking the sharp turns of the Pass like the devil's minions were chasing them.

The unmistakable form of Saxton with an axe in his hand could wait.

CHAPTER TWELVE

Ara slept for the next forty eight hours hardly moving on the bed. If Orelle didn't know what releasing a dragon entailed, she would have panicked and called Meredith away from the Gathering of Doyennes. Somewhere close to the 18th hour mark, Ara stirred, throwing away the new duvet Orelle had covered her with. Her arms and legs flailed as though pulled by strings. Her skin still had the mottled green, brown, and greys of her dragon but they were fading the longer she rested. She moaned incoherent sounds and drank every last drop of water, broth, or milk Orelle placed between her lips. Not once did she open her eyes.

Orelle stared out the window, still sat in the rocking chair beside Ara's bed. Whatever had Ara in its grip released her near dawn. Today was going to be a glorious day, but nothing felt springy or summery to her. The sun could have beat down on the garden or shone between the leaves of the trees for all its worth. All Orelle saw was disappointment in the blood red rosebushes that dotted the garden and the betrayal on the wings of so many birds that had nests in Havenshade's trees.

A soft knock preceded Meredith's arrival. She had her helmet under her arm and her jacket was open at the front showing an impeccable white chiffon blouse.

"How is she?" She took off the band that kept her hair up in a messy bun, allowing it to tumble around her shoulders. She walked to the side of Ara's bed gazing down in concern and gently feeling her forehead.

"She's good," Orelle said, setting aside the book she was reading on the bedside table as she stood. "Been sleeping all this time."

Meredith nodded before staring at her. "You look troubled."

"I'm fine." Orelle let go of the breath she didn't realise she held.

"Orelle…"

Even before she became Doyenne, Orelle already knew that Meredith had the uncanny ability of knowing when someone wasn't telling the truth. She swallowed the trepidation that deceptively landed on her chest like a blanket floating down to the ground.

"We were almost caught," Orelle hedged, hugging herself. "By slayers."

Meredith blanched, her pale skin becoming even paler.

"Outside," she said softly. All Orelle could hear was her dragon's roar.

By the time she reached the ground floor, Meredith already had the electric kettle on boil and two mugs with tea sachets created by Dragon magi. They were made of crushed cinnamon, ginger, and several other herbs meant to keep the beast inside them mellow. It also kept their scent hidden from slayers when they were in human form.

Orelle pulled out a chair and waited for Meredith to sit.

"I didn't expect Ara's foundling to moult this early," she said as she nodded her thanks when Meredith gently pushed a mug toward her.

"None of us do," Meredith said after taking a huge gulp of the boiling brew without a grimace.

Shit, she must really be pissed.

"Yes, I am but not at you," she quipped almost making Orelle sputter the tea to the table.

"Quit doing that!"

Meredith shrugged. Another mug of boiling tea and she finally sighed, almost in defeat.

"Can I talk now?"

She looked at Orelle. Sadness flitted across her mauve eyes before it disappeared. She nodded.

"Right," Orelle blew out a breath. "I texted Ara to say I was staying at my flat. When I came back here the house was quiet." She paused, waiting for a reaction. There was none. "I searched for her and when I arrived in her room she was beginning to moult so I had to take her to the reservoirs since the lake underneath isn't ready yet."

"Why water?" Meredith angled her head to the side.

"It was what Ara asked for," Orelle replied. "Remember she said she had an inkling her dragon's element was water? I asked for the cold earth to breathe when I first moulted. I took a page from there. She's a water dragon."

Interest lightened the dark flecks in Meredith's eyes before she became serious once more.

"Ara stayed in the reservoir for a long time." Orelle stood to get another helping of tea. "Then when she came out...Doyenne, she was beautiful. Her dragon is a brown diamond mixed with gold and green. And she is tall. Twenty feet for now but she'll grow." She remembered her first glimpse of Ara as she sliced through the water without making a sound. "I allowed her to frolic some more when she suddenly returned telling me that there were slayers nearby. I rushed her back here. You know the rest."

Meredith looked away with a troubled frown.

"There's something else, isn't there?"

Her question was spoken so softly that Orelle thought she was imagining it.

"Orelle?"

Orelle leaned against the counter, taking several huge gulps of the still hot should-not-gulp-tea-that-way brew. She became light headed the minute it hit her stomach, needing to take a few gulps of air to remove the sensation in her system.

Meredith didn't badger her, waiting until Orelle was ready to speak once more.

Orelle swallowed through the thickness threatening to close her throat.

"One of the slayers is someone I know."

"Oh Orelle."

"I didn't know he was a slayer, Doyenne." She threw her hands up, shaking her head vigorously.

Meredith stood making her third brew in the last hour.

Orelle worried her bottom lip. Meredith was furious if she was drinking the brew when once a day was more than enough.

"No Orelle, I'm not furious. I'm scared."

"Shit, Meredith. Stop doing that!"

"I'll let that pass because we are both raw and because you're one of my closest friends. As your Doyenne, and we are discussing matters that concern us all, never speak to me that way again."

Orelle's dragon cowered and lowered its head at the authority delivered in Meredith's deceptively soft voice. She fell to her knees, her head bowed.

"My apologies, Doyenne," she whispered. Fear trickled down her spine.

From underneath her lashes, she watched Meredith's heeled boots approach her. Her heart pounded, waiting for punishment. Instead, she heard her Doyenne sigh.

"Ahh shit, Orelle. Stand up. I can't do this."

Orelle heard the mug land down harder than normal on the table. She cringed.

"Orelle, come on!"

Carefully looking up, Orelle saw Meredith's troubled eyes looking at her.

"Never thought I'd see the day a Doyenne would plead with me."

"Don't push your luck."

Orelle mouthed 'Sorry' before she got up and sat on the chair.

"I can't help reading your thoughts when they're everywhere around you like speech bubbles," Meredith said.

"Is that how you know what people think?"

"Sometimes," she shrugged. "Other times I just know what someone is about to say." She squeezed Orelle's hand, her smile soft. "I'm sorry, Orelle. I didn't mean to pry."

This was the Meredith Orelle knew, the girl she grew up with. Orelle sensed her friend's anxiety and she didn't need to have ESP to know that her relationship with Saxton was the cause. Meredith made another cup of tea.

"Are you sure you want another one? You'll be stoned by the time we reach midday."

Meredith huffed a laugh. She filled the kettle once more. "I can take it. During training we were made to drink batches of this to see how much our dragons could tolerate."

"How much could you?" Curiosity about the secretive training of doyennes veered them away from their present worries.

"Twenty."

"No shit! I mean sorry, shit! Sorry Doyenne!" Orelle was doomed.

Meredith's tinkling laughter filled the room and she waved her hand in front of her face. Her other hand rested gently against her stomach.

"It's okay. I'm not using the Doyenne crap anymore while we talked now. Oh man." She couldn't stop giggling until it became full blow laughs that brought tears to her eyes.

"Yep, you're stoned." Orelle nodded, giggling because her friend was laughing.

"Right," Meredith gradually sobered. "About the slayer you know. Is it serious?"

"I thought it was until I found out he was one. Hey," Orelle scowled. "I though you said you'd stop reading minds."

"I didn't." Meredith's eyes widened and realization set in. "It is serious."

"I really don't know," Orelle almost whined. "Again why couldn't we have been given the ability to sense a slayer when we're human?"

"The same way slayers can't sense dragons when we're around people," Meredith replied. This time she sipped her tea even as far as blowing the steam away from the surface. "How did you hook up?"

Orelle rolled her eyes. Meredith's brow rose.

"I bumped into some friends and we went to a club."

"Something happened."

"Do we have to go into detail?" Orelle squirmed.

"We don't." Meredith shook her head.

Her voice was so soothing Orelle would probably tell her a blow by blow account of what happened to her and Saxton.

"Orelle, I really don't need to know details." Meredith shuddered then raised her hands defensively. "I can't help it!"

Orelle realized she should have taken that mental exercise of building a shield around her thoughts.

"Thank you!"

"Oh Lord, I think I better get another cup of tea."

Dusk had fallen and Orelle was nowhere near a solution to her problem with Saxton other than to avoid him at all costs. She didn't leave her number and hoped to God that while she was asleep he didn't riffle through the contents of her purse. Just the thought of giving him up made her restless, but if Saxton found out she was a dragon, he'd kill her.

Unless she killed him first.

The enmity between dragons and man had all but been lost in the fog of time before resurfacing as myths and legends. Orelle had lived long enough to know that there was a time when dragons were allowed to roam the land and be at peace with people. Some even fell in love with mortals and had families of their own. Then dragons had to be purged from the land when they became symbols of evil. Who gave dragons their false diabolical reputation in the first place was something Orelle wasn't familiar with. But what was evil, she mused. Was a man evil for killing another to protect his family? Meredith knew their history more than she did but the doyenne wasn't talking. All Orelle and Ara were instructed to do was to make sure that they didn't attract slayers. If slayers were found, they had to be killed.

Just the thought of ending Saxton's life made her chest tighten with misery. It made her want to wail and pull her hair in frustration. Even her beast was restless as though it didn't want to go into battle and kill the man who made Orelle happy.

Bullshit, he made her pussy happy.

Even as Orelle denied what Saxton was to her, she balked at her duty to end his life. It made the hole inside her chest big enough to encompass even her heart.

"I don't know what to do, Doyenne." Orelle sighed.

"You do," Meredith said. "It's right there in front of you. Thing is, you refuse to see it because your feelings run deeper than what it would have been had it just been a fling."

"Easier said than done," Orelle replied. Her brows creased. "What? I know that look, Mer. You're up to something."

A ghost of a smile passed through Meredith's lips.

"There's something I want to show you."

CHAPTER THIRTEEN

Orelle followed Meredith to Ara's potions room located at the back of the house.

"Are we making something stronger to drink?"

Meredith smiled enigmatically before walking to one of Ara's shelves filled with clean glass vials and bottles. She set aside a few of the bottles on the work counter and pressed her palm on the panelling. Orelle heard a loud click and Meredith stepped aside to swing the shelf outward to precede Orelle inside the secret corridor.

The whole time they had lived here, Orelle thought that she and Ara had found all of the unknown passageways that were just big enough should they suddenly change to their dragon forms. They never found this place Meredith had taken her to.

"Does Ara know about this?" Orelle was stupefied.

"She doesn't," Meredith replied. "I didn't know about it either until I became Doyenne." They reached a narrow vestibule where Meredith hit a switch.

Orelle drew in a sharp breath at the magnificence of the room. A long comfortable couch with lamps on each side was in the centre of a huge Aubusson.

Tables like the ones Orelle saw in Manchester's Central library lined the sides of the room. Gilded Klimts hobnobbed with Van Goghs, Renoirs, and Matisses on the cherry wood panelled walls. It was easy for Orelle to imagine clinking glasses of champagne, stage whispers of studious art discussions amid trays of canapés and the cloying perfumes of female art patrons. A spiral staircase in the corner of the room connected two more floors where shelves were filled with handstitched chronicles of Havenshade's dragons. Meredith didn't go up the stairwell in search of a particular volume. Instead, she proceeded to the centre wall on the main floor and put her palm once more against a square of granite. The rock glowed around her hand, a pulsing red as though the stone was being forged in fire before the light vanished and the sound of wood sliding against wood whispered in the still air.

"Looks too much of a cliché, don't you think?" Orelle couldn't stop the mockery in her voice.

Meredith glanced at her, her lips twisting to one side. "Look around you, Orelle. We are living in a world built on clichés."

Orelle shook her head. Bewilderment was an under word as opposed to an understatement. "I didn't even know there was a place like this inside Havenshade."

"You're not supposed to know that we do." Meredith's voice was strained as she took out a giant volume out of the compartment. She sneezed after blowing some of the dust from the top cover. She placed the tome on the table flanked by the sofas. "Doyennes become the keepers of their lair's chronicles. Unless really necessary, they have the prerogative whether to reveal its presence or not. Especially when they feel that one of them is in danger."

Orelle ceased her awed perusal of her surroundings. She frowned.

"In danger of what?"

"Of falling in love with their slayer."

Orelle stared at her friend.

"What?" Meredith asked, heaving more than half of the volume open. "Make yourself some coffee or tea. It's over there." She indicated the small coffee counter with her head.

Orelle stood just to get away from something uncomfortable. "You sound as though this has happened before." There were several pods for her choose from. After the tea in the kitchen, she needed something bitter that would keep her alert. She inserted the espresso pod at the same time setting a demi-tasse underneath the spout and waited.

"Yes it has." Meredith replied quietly. "I'd like a latté please."

"When?" Orelle took out her demi-tasse, replacing it with Meredith's latté glass. She leaned her hip against the counter.

"All in good time."

Orelle's lips thinned. Leave it to Meredith to be cryptic. She had those moments even when they were children.

Demi-tasse and latté glass in hand, Orelle set them down on the table. Sitting down beside her friend, she was aghast at the name Meredith pointed at.

Chandra Varma.

"But that's —"

"My predecessor? Yes."

Orelle leaned away.

"No way." She gazed at Meredith's face trying to find the truth...hell even just some form truth would be nice even if it started with a lie. "That's impossible! She would have been killed! The Gathering would have condemned her to die and the slayer would remain earth bound for the rest of his God forsaken life!"

"She was condemned. On the day of her execution, someone busted her out of her prison cell. A magus placed a binding spell so that she couldn't transform but after leaving her cell, she went to the caves and shifted, flying away with the one who saved her."

"Her slayer?"

"I honestly don't know. Could be," Meredith answered after taking one huge gulp of her latté. "We didn't know where she was. We didn't care to either. But word got around. Months later someone found Chandra's body by a road leading to Cardiff."

Orelle remembered Havenshade's previous doyenne. She remembered the sparkle of mischief in Chandra's thickly lashed eyes and the shine of her blacker than black hair. She had been a black dragon, whose scales and even the tips of her horns shimmered with an iridescent violet when light hit them. Air had been her element. She also had a motherly aura even though she had only been a hundred years older than Orelle, Meredith, and Ara. But Orelle had remembered that a few months before Chandra disappeared from Havenshade, she had been withdrawn. She kept to the living room looking out at the skies. She kept her eyes lowered until Orelle spied her once and she couldn't understand how sadness and joy could mix so completely in someone's eyes. It was Orelle's most enduring memory. Chandra's death struck a chord in her that unleashed a powerful wave of fury from her and her beast.

She forced herself not to squirm in her seat at Meredith's sudden cool glare. It was difficult to think that her friend was still her friend.

"This thing you have with the slayer has to stop, Orelle. I can tolerate almost anything you and Ara do, but not this."

"Doyenne, I didn't even know he was a slayer until I saw him with the other slayer in Ladybower. Surely you can't pin that fault on me. And now that I know what happened to Chandra, and who Saxton is, I won't see him again."

Meredith stared at her that made Orelle want the floor to open up underneath her.

"Good." Meredith finally said, relieved then gave her an assessing look. "You want to ask me something?"

"How do you know?"

"How do I know what?"

"Not you, you," Orelle clarified. "You as in general. How does a dragon know who the slayer is?"

Meredith leaned against the arm rest of the couch. She had that faraway look that Orelle saw only once. Years ago.

"What happens between you and Saxton?"

Orelle scowled, flushing.

Meredith rolled her eyes. "That's not what I meant." She paused. Her eyes narrowed to slits in trying to find the right words. "When you're with him, does he take your breath away?"

Orelle's face cleared remembering Saxton's kisses. She sighed and nodded. "Yes."

"Literally?"

"Yes." Orelle was bemused now.

"And when you come together –"

"Meredith!"

Meredith's face softened. "It was different, wasn't it? And something moved inside you, peeling itself away from the surface of your heart."

Orelle looked away. How different could it get? Just because making love with Saxton brought her to heights beyond everything she knew didn't mean she couldn't find it with someone else.

Point was, she didn't want to be with anyone else.

Being with Saxton was like seeing the world in a brighter light. Just watching him softened her heart and she wouldn't be surprised if it became as soft as a pillow. His smile made her melt, his laugh tickled her insides until her stomach did somersaults and her pulse became as fast as a hummingbird's wings. His eyes…oh Lord…when he devoured her with those grey green pools, she could be a puddle at his feet. When Saxton took her, Orelle thought she'd burst with the intensity of her climax that she felt she could touch the stars and feel the fiery blaze of the sun scorch her own soul. And when she fell back to earth, a sense of loss seeped into her bones knowing that she and Saxton were no longer one. No matter how sore her body was, she couldn't get enough of him. She couldn't stop him from taking her breath away over and over again until she gave it willingly. Every time he did that, the floating surface encircling her heart wanted to seep out of her.

And into Saxton.

No man had made her feel that way. There was one relationship in the past that nearly broke her. What she had with Saxton could tear her apart.

"I won't see him again." Orelle looked at her demi-tasse as though it was the most interesting thing in the world. She owed it to her kind. There would be other men.

But there wouldn't be anyone like Saxton.

"It's not that."

Orelle looked at Meredith. "Excuse me?"

Meredith looked at her without really seeing her. "It's not that you won't see him again. You will. You won't be able to help it."

Orelle's chin lifted. "Do you think I don't have

136

the willpower to do so?"

Meredith shook her head, her eyes sad.

The demi-tasse landed on the coffee table with a bang. Orelle stood, her eyes blazing.

"How dare you?"

"Sit down."

"That's not fair, Mer. You switch to being the Doyenne when it pleases you. And yet you said earlier you'd set that aside."

"I'm not your doyenne now." Meredith didn't flinch. "I'm just telling you the truth. You will not be able to resist Saxton even if you tried."

"Why because we fucked and he took my breath away, literally?"

"Yes."

"So what?"

"Taking your breath into him was his way of taking what truly belongs to him."

The sinking feeling in Orelle's stomach went straight down to her feet.

"You're the keeper of his soul. His Omega," Meredith said. "And he's your destined slayer."

CHAPTER FOURTEEN

"I could have maimed it." Braden sulked. "Had we arrived sooner we would have seen who helped the dragon get away."

"We don't know if it was the dragon and a sympathiser or a horny couple we disturbed," Saxton said. He had his back to his fellow slayers as he narrowed his gaze at the dark waters of the reservoir.

"Horny my hairy arse." Braden snorted. "Lots of horns."

"Whose did it belong to?" Owen was deep in thought.

Each slayer answered a particular dragon's call like one of Ulysses' men longing for the siren's song. When a slayer didn't feel a burn in his gut upon seeing a dragon, then he could only injure and not kill it. Killing the dragon was an honour that belonged to the slayer who heard that call. Taking out an Omega was enough to cause a rift between slayers that could never be repaired because it would keep the slayer in some sort of limbo for the rest of his earthly life.

"It was Jason's Omega." Saxton turned around.

Theo's brow rose. "Mine? And you know this because?"

"Gut feel."

Theo snickered. "Next time, I'll make sure I'm

here to see if you're right. Don't want to kill someone else's dragon and make an enemy for life."

"Gut feel is what we use most of the time to stay alive." Saxton shrugged.

"When there were still more dragons stupid enough to come out during the day. It's been centuries since that's happened," Derrick opined as he perched on the side sofa's arm rest. "We must be losing our touch."

"You're a jackass." Braden grumbled.

"I'm just saying!" Derrick gestured with his hands. "Tell me, when was the last time you slew a dragon that wasn't your Omega? Let alone have seen the dragon you were meant to kill?"

Braden's brows pulled together.

"My point exactly," Derrick said, winking. Braden looked at him oddly.

Saxton watched the slayers. Derrick was right. Dragons rarely showed themselves and with every passing year, decade, or century, the slayers lived longer, trapped in a world where life only had superficial meaning.

"We'll take turns patrolling." Saxton moved away from the French doors. "Theo, want to have first dibs?"

Theo nodded, his face sober.

"I'll join you." Braden rose from the couch. "I can show you where we last saw it and find some clues."

"Good," Saxton said. "Owen we might as well extend camera range all the way to the end of the reservoir. Can our tech handle it?"

"I'll make it so." Owen strode away from them taking the stairs leading to the basement.

"Right, I'm heading back to the bar," Derrick said standing. "Sabine's going to whip my hide if I stay here any longer. We're three people down on the floor."

All of them heard Owen's growl from the basement. They all chuckled.

"Sorry, bro. You're the tech expert. I'm just a slayer," Derrick drawled in amusement. "Besides, Sabine asked specifically for me."

"Get the hell out!"

When everyone left in the midst of guffaws at Owen's expense, Saxton went to the kitchen to brew some coffee. While the espresso's notes joined the air he breathed, he puzzled over the fact that Orelle's scent became stronger the closer they were to the dragon's position. Alarm bells had his gut wringing tight as he watched the Sirocco speed away. As sharp as his eyes were, he couldn't see the person hunkered down in the driver's seat. Was the person the dragon in human form? Or was the dragon inside the car?

He took his drink with him out to the patio once more. The four wheel drive Theo and Braden took bounced over the hilly road, the tail lights looking like a dragon's red eyes lying in wait for its unsuspecting prey. Saxton's thoughts returned to Orelle.

After their lovemaking, she had left him content yet wanting more at the same time. Each moment of passion flaring between them drew him closer to her. She was a temptress. Saxton couldn't explain why every time he took in her breath, clarity followed but he liked that. What he didn't care for was that his moral compass and his judgement were being tested. He never knew what guilt was, never knew what pity or compassion for dragons were. It didn't bother him that the dragons, in their human form may have left families behind. Now it somehow did. He was developing a conscience so late in life. It troubled him now that he had killed many dragons during training in preparation of finally vanquishing his Omega. It disturbed him now to realize that there would be children not growing up with a father or a mother, a brother, a sister. A best friend. This uncomfortable feeling made Saxton shift from one foot to the other. It made him want to get out of his own skin.

All because he had put his axes against a dragon's neck or pierced the heart beating underneath its scales. Or that he had pursued a wounded dragon in its human form who, marred by the wound already inflicted on it, would never be able to escape death. As slayers, men like him were as vicious as they were cruel. But dragons were only defending themselves.

What. The. Fuck?

Damn Orelle for making him feel and fall. But he wouldn't have it any other way. He couldn't wait to get her back in his bed and in his arms, not because he needed to be inside her. That was just part of the equation. He couldn't bear to be away from her now for even a second. He was starting to need her with a desperation that was beginning to worry him. She was an addiction and an obsession all rolled into one beautiful person whose smile was brighter than a diamond under bright lights and whose laughter was like the tinkling of chimes that soothed his weary heart. He didn't have her number. He never asked for women's numbers. Now he regretted that he didn't ask for hers at all. Shit. He was becoming addled because Orelle had come into his life making him forget his soulless existence.

Maybe if he stayed longer with Orelle, he wouldn't need to kill his dragon.

Something inside him locked into place – a realisation that he might be able to find a semblance of his soul in another person. He didn't need to die to find peace and leave this wretched life. Not when Orelle was there.

He didn't see the necessity of having to kill his Omega either. A weight he didn't realise he had been carrying lifted from his chest.

"Owen!" He stormed back into the farm house.

"Yeah!" Owen's head peeked out by the basement stairs.

"I need you to do something for me."

* * *

By the time Saxton arrived in Orelle's flat, he was in a state of agitation. Derrick had given him Orelle's credit card details which Owen in turn tracked. All three slayers hid it from Sabine because if she knew, shit would hit the fan. Their waitress and bouncer was a stickler for data protection shit. Derrick wasn't exactly jumping up and down either only because he didn't want Sabine's boot up his behind.

It was now 2:00 am. The windows of Orelle's apartment were pitch black. Save for a few windows with dimmed lights. Saxton spied a mobile of angels and wings silently and slowly circling over a crib. It suddenly jerked to wakefulness when he heard a baby's wails. The mother, hair dishevelled came into view, bending over before standing with the baby in her arms. She swung around in a slow tempo, kissing her child who was moving in consternation of having to wake up.

Saxton felt an intense pang of loneliness that he had to rub the ache away from his chest. He suddenly had a longing to put down roots and have someone whom he could pass down his legacy to. He wanted someone beside him who'd share his life, become his whole world, and grow old with. Until slayers reclaimed their souls, they remained young. Slayers were allowed to mate with anyone they deemed worthy and when they had to confess what they did, their chosen mates had to swear an oath of secrecy. Saxton hadn't found anyone worthy...

Until Orelle came along.

He looked up once more. Mother and child had long gone. The stillness of the night that blanketed the block of red bricked apartments gave way to the first blush of the morning. Saxton eased his muscular frame out of the Audi A6. Darkness still pervaded Orelle's apartment as though no one was home. Saxton frowned. Orelle told him she was going home when they parted. Where was she? Doubt wriggled its way inside his mind, its demonic horns glittering and sharp. Was she hurt? Her apartment wasn't far from The Brew Bar. Had he known, he would have taken her home but Orelle was adamant that she be allowed to leave on her own. His stomach slowly bottomed out.

Was she hiding someone?

Saxton's jaw clenched. A green eyed dragon reared its ugly head taunting him and he couldn't do shit unless he wanted to commit hara kiri and pull it out of his gut like Ridley Scott's Alien. His eyes narrowed at a woman rushing to leave the gated block of flats.

"Ahh you saved me the bother of getting my own keys," he said rushing to hold the gate open much to the surprise and interest of the woman. Saxton turned on the charm. She, on the other hand, swept her delicately kohl rimmed eyes over his body, a smile crooking her lips.

"Late night?" her voice was sultry. If Orelle hadn't turned his life upside down in a span of just a few weeks, he wouldn't have hesitated to invite this woman back to her own apartment where she could scream the entire block down as he fucked her. He nodded instead.

"Heavy night at the bar."

She cocked her head to one side. "You're not

from around here."

"New neighbour," he said. "Moved in two weeks ago."

"Really?" She moved in, her long silky hair falling over her shoulder "I'm Beata. I'm in 4B. Call on me when you're not busy. I'd love to welcome you to the building."

Saxton grinned as leaned down and whispered in her ear. "I'm sure you do."

Beata beamed at him, blushing before walking away.

He wiped his smile as he efficiently entered the building, taking the fire exit two steps at a time. No point in alerting the rest of the tenants if he encountered any in the lift. Owen said that each floor only had two flats and Orelle lived on the fifth floor. Exiting the stairwell, Saxton honed his senses on the occupant of the other flat. A smile shadowed his mouth when he heard the woman screaming like she was in a rodeo.

Saxton knocked at Orelle's door. His mouth quirked. He was sure Orelle would be surprised when she opened the door. He'd deal with the fall out if Orelle got angry at him. She might even accuse him of stalking. Guilty.

He knocked again. No answer. His senses tingled. Something was wrong. Just as he was about to pick the lock, Orelle's neighbour came out.

"Hi," Saxton greeted. "I was supposed to meet Orelle for breakfast but she didn't arrive."

"How did you get in?" Orelle's neighbour eyed

him suspiciously.

"Look, mate. I'm sorry. A tenant allowed me in to check on Orelle." Okay, technically that was stretching a bit. "I'm just really worried about her. You want my name? Saxton Lance."

"Whatever." Orelle's neighbour waved his hand dismissively. "She isn't in."

"She didn't come home?" Saxton's brow pulled together.

"She doesn't stay here all the time, only during school time. She doesn't stay often even then." The neighbour volunteered. "I can tell you she didn't come home last night. I had a party and knocked to invite her. No answer."

"Okay, thanks." Saxton pulled out a card from his light jacket. "Here. Drop by the bar anytime. Your first meal's on me."

The neighbour's face cleared. "The Brew Bar? I've heard good things about the place. Thanks!"

"Cheers, mate."

Orelle's neighbour closed his door. Saxton left through the fire exit once more his mind roiling, his heart nearly bottoming out.

Where the hell is she?

CHAPTER FIFTEEN

Orelle switched the engine off. The faint scent of petrol fumes tickled her nose inside the basement parking lot. Pulling her purse from the passenger seat towards her, she got out, beeping the car lock on her way to the lift. College was starting soon. She needed time out from dealing with Ara's moulting to focus on her day job, and take her mind off Saxton. Good thing she dropped by the carwash to remove the vestiges of her trip to the reservoirs. Orelle closed her eyes as she leaned against the lift. The soft hum signalled her ascent to the fifth floor, the pipe in classical music soothing her tired muscles.

Thank God, Saxton didn't know about this place.

Orelle worried her bottom lip. Chalk it up to experience for not knowing a slayer from a regular guy. Before everything had gone pear-shaped with Ara, she already started entertaining thoughts of taking what she had with Saxton to a deeper level. She didn't have any delusions that it wouldn't go the other way either. Saxton was the only one who made her body come alive. Desire consumed her when he was around. He lit her up when she thought there couldn't be any other area of pleasure they hadn't both discovered. Even her beast had surrendered, retreating to the recesses of Orelle's psyche content

147

to curl around itself.

Now that she knew what Saxton was, the only way Orelle could describe what her beast was doing was…lamenting. There was this huge ball of regret in the centre of her chest that increased the emptiness she was starting to feel.

"Fifth floor," the disembodied voice of the lift announced. Straightening away from the lift's wall, she stepped out only to be greeted by her neighbour and a girl Orelle noticed was different from the one she met the last time.

"Geez, you startled me." She laughed, her hand on her chest.

"Hey Orelle." Her neighbour nudged his chin in greeting. "Dave."

"Yes, Dave. Sorry."

Dave waved his hand dismissively while his girl de jour smiled at Orelle. "You're hardly here so no big deal."

They allowed her to get off before they entered the lift.

"Oh by the way, you had a visitor here this morning," Dave said.

"Oh really?"

"Yeah. Said you were supposed to meet for breakfast. Saxophone or something."

The phantom sucker punch came out of nowhere making Orelle blink repeatedly. "Saxton."

"Yeah, that's the one," Dave replied not noticing Orelle's distress.

"Oh yes." She feigned a sigh. "I had an

emergency and couldn't get any signal where I was."

Dave's forehead puckered in concern. "Everything all right?"

"Everything's fine." Orelle took her keys out of her purse. "My younger sister caught a bug and my older sister was away in London so…" she left it at that partial truth. "Thanks anyway. I'll text him now that I'm back."

The moment the lift closed, Orelle rushed to her flat. The panic she staved off while talking to Dave slammed into her in full force and made her crumple to the floor. She began to hyperventilate, terror gripping her. Saxton knew where she lived! Her beast unfurled. Knowing that Saxton was its destined slayer didn't sit well.

She looked around the cream walls with tiny silk creations of an Oriental artist living in Hong Kong and the overstuffed paisley sofa ensemble. She looked at the huge kitchen with its wood and chrome finishing – her joy and place where she whipped up her favourite dishes.

Her place of Zen had been sullied by a dragonslayer. Slow burning fury replaced all the emotions that made her want to cower. Her pulse thudded hard in her temples, her wrists, the base of her neck. Heat from the dragon's fire inside her seeped through her eyes and a soft snarl came from her throat.

How dare Saxton come uninvited? More than that, how the hell did he know? She had been careful not to leave any trace. She checked her phone for security breaches. None. Why the hell did he have to spoil her sanctuary with his presence?

Why indeed? If things were different would she have been thrilled that Saxton had stalker tendencies? She would never know as disappointment and anger clouded her thinking.

Orelle braced herself on all fours. A series of hot and cold flashes went through her like the blinking lights of a red light district beer garden. She didn't know which was worse – knowing who Saxton was or Saxton knowing where she lived. She stiffened. Had Saxton seen her driving away? Had he started tracking her down? Orelle stood, her eyes still burning with her dragon's fire which could incinerate anyone in a matter of seconds. She looked around at everything she had worked so hard for. In a matter of minutes the walls became impersonal, the paintings became mere fixtures to showcase the flat's spaciousness. What the hell. She hardly lived in it anyway.

She entered her bedroom and took the suitcase down from above the wardrobe. Drawers were opened, clothes dumped into the suitcase, and phone secured between Orelle's ear and shoulder.

"Halton Properties? Hi." She folded a pair of jeans. "I want to sell my flat as soon as possible, please. My name's Orelle Molyneux. Yes...you sold me the property....How long before..."

She continued talking and packing, each word and piece of clothing symbolic of severing the long stretch of attachment she had with the place she had considered her second home. Each word, a welt of betrayal and resignation.

She may live a somewhat normal life.

It just didn't mean she was normal.

CHAPTER SIXTEEN

Saxton tried Orelle's phone for the umpteenth time without success.

"Are you sure this is her number?" He scowled at Owen who was lounging on the sofa of The Brew Bar office.

"Course, I'm sure. That's what her geo tracker showed." Owen continued chewing on a toothpick. "Here take a look." Sitting up, he typed a series of letters and turned the laptop around for Saxton to view.

Saxton didn't bother. He was feeling suddenly warm and sweat was starting to form in the centre of his chest and his armpits.

"What's easy for you is gibberish for us mortal men."

Owen grunted. "Semi mortal. If you were mortal, you wouldn't be a stud at five hundred years old. No one would give you the time of day unless you're a billionaire about to croak."

"Shut up." Saxton grumbled feeling uncharacteristically warm.

"What I don't get, Apollo, is why you're so hung up on Orelle."

"Find another one," Theo volunteered. "We can go back to the club where you met her. There will be dozens like her there and you can take your pick."

"They're not her," Saxton muttered, pulling at his short hair. His temperature was rising and he felt like he was going to internally combust. Plus, his search for Orelle was becoming an obsession. Why? He didn't have a fucking clue.

"Then Dude, she might just be the one for you." Theo's eyes were filled with sympathetic amusement.

"And if I die killing my dragon?"

Neither Theo nor Owen spoke, only knowing too well that the same fate lay for them as slayers.

"The best thing to do is probably wait." Theo suggested. "If she doesn't return then she doesn't and you have to move on."

Saxton couldn't even consider the thought. "I'm going back to the flat."

"That's stalking let alone harassment." Owen's face hardened, his lazy demeanour incrementally disappearing.

"Then where the hell can I find her?" Saxton shouted. Everyone in the room stiffened in shock, including him. "Shit, I don't know what's happening."

He couldn't understand his irrational need to find Orelle. He could feel something shrivelling inside him, an agonising pain blooming in the center of his chest. The pain intensified with every beat of his heart and only Orelle could fix it. Saxton didn't know where that idea came from but he just knew that he was right.

"What the hell's wrong with you man?" Owen

stood, his arms gesturing to the sides in confusion.

"Bloody hell, Sax, you're burning up." Theo took his hand away from Saxton's shoulder, baffled.

Saxton wanted to go quietly out of his mind.

It's just the fever. Just the fever making me go haywire. Orelle can fix this.

There was a knock before Sabine entered.

"Jesus, you look awful." She wrinkled her nose. "And what's that smell?"

"I don't smell anything." Owen scoffed.

"I'm not surprised. You're nose blind." Sabine said in disdain.

Owen crossed his arms over his chest. His eyes roamed Sabine's body lazily.

"Like you would know."

Sabine rolled her eyes. Her scowl looked as though she could siphon out the lights in the office. She pointed at Saxton. "You have –"

"Orelle." Saxton stormed out of the office.

"Hey!" Sabine stepped aside otherwise Saxton would have mowed her down.

He was a man on a mission, crazed because he couldn't get his fix. Orelle's scent wafted through the corridor and with every breath he took, a little bit of his fever subsided like a misty rain cooling him. Soft. Soothing. Saxton's hand flattened against the wall. He wasn't as crazed as he was earlier but he now felt an ache consuming his body and crushing his bones.

"Saxton, hold up!" Theo followed, exasperation in his voice. He darted a glance at the bar. "You're in no condition to deal with her. I'll do it."

"No," Saxton roared but it came out as a croak. "I need to see her. Hold her. Can bring…this …fever…down."

"How do you know that?" Theo gritted, half in exasperation and disbelief. "You've just met her."

Saxton didn't bother to reply. If Orelle's scent had tamed the storm inside him, it was logical that she might bring the fever down as well. Each step he made was an effort to do. When he entered the bar, Orelle was by the door. She looked furious but when she saw him, astonishment froze her. Then worry clouded her face. Thank God, there weren't any diners. It was the lull before the bar opened to patrons. Orelle strode to him and the moment she neared, Saxton leaned on to her.

"You're burning up!" she gasped. She looked at Theo. "What happened?"

"You tell me." Theo's voice dripped with sarcasm. "He's been like that since you disappeared."

Saxton wanted to wipe off his face. But how could he when he could hardly lift his arm.

"I didn't disappear and it's not like we're joined at the hip." She gave him a withering glare. "What's with you?

"Orelle…help…me." Saxton murmured, his lungs deflating.

It was the last thing he did before darkness took over.

* * *

Sleeping with the enemy was one thing. Entering

their lair without backup was stupid. Orelle was furious that Saxton invaded her privacy and it was taking all of her strength to rein in a seething dragon and not unleash it in the middle of a bar. The bar was going to be the scene of a bloodbath if any of the slayers got a whiff of her dragon. Then again, it might not. How would the men explain killing a customer in cold blood? Self-defense by reason of a dragon's presence? In the middle of the city? They'd all be kicked into the slammer and considered insane. She was sorely tempted to goad them, especially Theo who questioned her as if she was responsible for Saxton's delirium. Owen's face was stony but not accusatory. Both slayers carried Saxton up to the third floor.

"You better go up, too." Sabine whispered, a smile shadowing her mouth. "Saxton belongs to you."

Orelle turned to face Sabine but the girl left before she could ask what she meant. She took the stairs slowly, the old steps creaking under her weight. The door to Saxton's room was open and she saw Theo and Owen on each side of the bed where Saxton lay bathed in his sweat.

"Orelle…"

She winced when pain streaked across the surface of her heart. It was as if the space around the organ was slowly being peeled away once more. Theo turned to her, his face grim. Orelle waited warily as he approached. His eyes were like flint, his hands clenched and worry covered his face.

"This is the first time that this has happened to him." He exhaled deeply. "Help Saxton...please."

If Orelle didn't have feelings for Saxton beyond their satisfying physical tussle, she wouldn't have agreed to Theo's request.

"I wish I could but I don't know how." She rubbed her arms to remove the sudden chill that descended as she stared at Saxton.

"Stay with him as long as you can." Theo said following Orelle's gaze. "He seems to calm down when you're around."

"And he's edgy when I'm not?" Orelle huffed a laugh. Theo's hard gaze pinned her.

"He has been searching for you since you left," he said.

That makes things more complicated.

"I'll do my best."

Theo and Owen left her, the latter's mouth curving apologetically. Orelle walked to the bed. Sweat plastered Saxton's hair to his scalp. His shirt was drenched.

She sat down on the edge of the bed. Saxton looked at her with fever glazed eyes that darkened his irises with a nearly unholy light. Orelle winced. The thin thread that held the film to her heart pulled – a sore reminder no different from the most painful sunburn.

"What happened, Sax?"

"I don't know," he said. "This fever...it won't go away. You can make it go away."

She frowned in consternation. "How? I don't

know what brought it on."

Saxton heaved a long sigh. His stomach remained curved and Orelle was about to nudge him when he took an indrawn breath. She felt powerless to help him. She really didn't know what to do. Who would have thought her heart would squeeze painfully at seeing a dragonslayer so vulnerable? She could kill him right now and leave quickly. She had the advantage, didn't she? But she couldn't do it. Just the thought of killing him made bile rise up her throat. Her entire body wanted to weep. Even her beast stayed coiled inside her, not wanting to fight a slayer weakened by a malady they knew nothing of.

Saxton grabbed her wrist when she stood. An electric current surged through her arm flicking the switch of her libido inside her. Saxton groaned in longing and Orelle felt it too. The ache, the hunger and the need to be with him was an exquisite agony. She knew her heart was bleeding, could feel it. She could imagine it dripping blood now that the film around it had completely broken away and was just hanging on by a thread. Yet she knew that it had to be this way. Some ingrained sense told her that Saxton needed what her heart was letting go. It was the only way he could rid himself of the fever.

"I need to get a towel from the bathroom," she said, her voice hoarse. Pain and pleasure at his touch rushed through her.

"I can't let you go."

Like Newton's apple falling from the tree, Orelle realized that she couldn't let Saxton suffer. She was

Saxton's Omega. And as the keeper of his soul she had to die to give him his life. Her eyes misted as that knowledge settled softly over her. Her heart had kept Saxton's soul long before they knew each other until it was time to return it. It also dawned on her that the man she had fallen in love with was the very person who had injured her the last time she ventured to the woods.

"I won't let you let me go," she said softly, caressing his heated skin. "The towel, Sax. You're sweating a river."

Saxton struggled to sit up. His breathing was harsh as he swung his legs over the edge of the bed.

"Shower...with me." He stood and leaned against Orelle. His eyes blazed with fever and lust, darkening to almost black. "Now."

Desire bloomed with an answering pulse beating in the apex of Orelle's thighs. Yes, she would give Saxton this last time. She'd give herself this last chance to feel the what-could-have-been before the what-must-be was allowed to pierce her bubble of happiness.

Orelle's fingers interlaced with Saxton's and she pulled him slowly towards the bathroom. She helped him remove his clothes before she removed hers. Their breathing was laboured and expectant. Saxton's fevered gaze devoured every inch of her naked body as her own gaze roamed his golden skin. He stepped closer and Orelle welcomed him in her arms, her mouth seeking his in a kiss of fire that threatened to consume her. Saxton's touch scorched and pleased her. There was no finesse in the way they came together, no benefit of foreplay. Because the moment she turned on the tap, Saxton turned her around to face the wall, held her hips and rubbed his hot and thick erection against her ass before dipping against her moist opening. She cried out, trying to grip the slippery wall when Saxton thrust into her. The shock sent ripples of unexpected pleasure to her sex, her liquid heat coating Saxton's cock and she clamped around him.

She closed her eyes as her body submitted to Saxton's thrusts her body reaching that moment when she's explode in sheer pleasure. This was where she wanted to be. This was how she wanted to be taken. This was the man she wanted, who consumed her with his kisses and his body.

The dragonslayer tasked with ending her life.

* * *

Orelle donned her blouse as she slowly got out of bed. She turned at the waist to look at Saxton's sleeping form. He had been insatiable, taking everything she gave and giving her what her heart and body desired. She swallowed and couldn't stop the sad smile forming on her lips, her throat feeling scratchy from her orgasms. Just as Saxton predicted, his fever subsided. His skin wasn't as hot and flushed. His features had softened in sleep. His chest and sculpted stomach moved as he breathed. No blanket covered his form, allowing Orelle her fill of drinking his magnificence. Saxton's body was perfection that Orelle just wanted to lie down again and put her head on his chest. The moment they came together, Saxton allowed her to reach the stars and join them. She was the air he breathed. He was her desire. But she was a dragon and he, her slayer. They were enemies from the get go and no amount of tactical diplomacy would change what was destined to happen.

Kill or be killed.

She got up slowly, wincing inwardly at every time the floor creaked under her feet. She gathered the rest of her clothes and pocketed her panties which Saxton had torn in his frenzy to put his mouth on her when Orelle had started to dress up after their steamy shower. Her core clenched once more at the memory of that desperation.

Saxton mumbled. Orelle whirled around but he continued to sleep, in fact, turning away from her. She moved to the bedside table and scribbled a note for him on the pad. After she finished, she stared at him once more. The lamp cast light and shadow on his face. Saxton's breathing was easier and a faint contented smile shadowed his mouth.

Anguish was starting to make Orelle's emotions choppy. Soon she needed to brace for the tidal wave that would surely drown her. Saxton gave her one of the best experiences of her life – what it was like to experience ecstasy. And heartbreak. Many would think that she was a fool. Hell, she thought herself all kinds of stupid for falling for the very person who had to kill her in order to live to a ripe old age then die.

But wasn't that what life was all about? Sacrifice?

Pulling herself away from her state of becoming-philosophical-to-justify-maudlin thoughts, Orelle forced her gaze away from Saxton and walked towards the door. She was playing a dangerous game by leaving him a message. It didn't matter. She had already compromised herself. She couldn't let her sister dragons suffer because of what she had done. She had to protect them.

Orelle held her shoes in one hand as she slipped out of the room. She traversed the third floor corridor, hoping that she wouldn't see anyone so she could slip out the back door.

No such bloody luck.

Theo and Owen were talking to Sabine on the opposite side of the hallway when Orelle emerged.

"Leaving?" Theo sauntered towards her.

"He's fine, thanks for asking." Orelle's brow slightly puckered. She bristled at Theo's tone. "It's not like Saxton's fever is my fault."

Theo backed down, hands up and palms raised. He exhaled raking a hand through his blond hair and dry rubbing his face.

"That was uncalled for." He nodded.

"Was that supposed to be an apology? If that's all I can get, I'll take it." Orelle let her boots fall to the floor and slipped her feet into them.

"Why are you leaving?" Theo's blue eyes assessed her, his head cocked to the side.

"Because this has to end." She busied herself zipping her ankle boots so Theo didn't see how much it cost her to say those words.

"Care to tell me why?"

Sabine and Owen watched them. Orelle didn't care. She needed to get what she thought out of her chest.

"Saxton invaded my privacy." She said on a breath, her forehead furrowing "There was a reason why I didn't let him have my number or why I didn't tell him where I lived. That was what I came to tell him before you demanded that I do something about his fever. Now that it's done, I'm leaving."

"Orelle –"

"It's not like we're together, Theo." Impatience crept into her hoarse voice. "It's done."

"But you feel something for him as he does for you."

She stared at him, surprised at the sudden gentleness of his tone. At that moment, her eyes turned to Sabine who stared at her in shock. Was that recognition in her eyes? There was more to it, as though Sabine knew her truth. Then Sabine pivoted rushing back to the dining area leaving a puzzled Owen alone.

"I have to go." The last thing Orelle wanted was for Saxton to wake up while she was still there.

"He will want to talk to you," Theo said.

Orelle let out a bitter chuckle. "Maybe, but I don't think that's going to happen."

"Orelle –"

"Goodbye, Theo."

She pushed at the back door and let herself out into the finally warm night. After the cold rain of the past days, the warmth was a welcome respite.

It just wasn't enough to help thaw the ice around her heart.

CHAPTER SEVENTEEN

Orelle sat inside her car for the longest time, looking at Havenshade's façade. She couldn't find it in herself to cry even as her heart continued to break. There was no way in Heaven or Hell that she and Saxton could be together and because of this, she saw her life slipping away. Sure, she could always hide or even move to another country. Selling her flat started the ball rolling. But Saxton would find her. He'd search the ends of the earth for her. She let out a mirthless laugh. Dramatic and an absolute cliché that stated the truth. The only way to stop him was to battle it out with him where there could only be one victor.

One dead slayer.

Or one very dead dragon.

The entrance door opened and light spilled out from behind Meredith. She didn't approach Orelle. Neither did Orelle expect her to. They stared at each other through the windshield before Meredith slightly nodded and returned inside the manor, leaving the door ajar.

Orelle got out of the car and lugged out the huge suitcase from the baggage compartment. She pulled it behind her, the wheels rolling over the courtyard's crushed shell and pebble surface. Leaving her suitcase in the foyer, she closed the entrance door, her eyes automatically looking at the ancient chandelier that glittered with Swarovski crystals. The lights inside the house welcomed her as it had always done since the time she became part of the Havenshade Dragons sisterhood. It was no different from a sorority house except that their membership was dwindling while a sorority's increased. She entered the living room that had given her so many hours of reading pleasure. Ara was there, still looking weak but there was more colour on her pale as onion skin cheeks.

"Hi Orelle," Ara greeted her with a wan but happy smile. "Pretty cool, huh? I'm a water dragon. Who would have thought? Thank you for saving my life and that of my foundling."

Orelle rushed to her when Ara made an effort to get up from her comfy place on the couch.

"You don't have to stand yet," Orelle said before kneeling down to embrace her friend. "You're welcome. Good thing I arrived when I did. Should you already be out of your room? And what's that awful smell?"

"That awful smell," Ara pointed to her cup. "Is what has allowed me to get out in the first place."

"Can't you put a little cinnamon or something to make it more nose friendly? It stinks like an alley filled with all sorts of vomit."

Ara's face brightened. "You just gave me an idea."

Orelle groaned but smiled and looked lovingly at

the beautiful face of her dragon sister. The tears she refused to shed when she left The Brew Bar welled and spilled from her eyes. Ara's face fell.

"Orelle, what gives?"

"She's met her slayer."

Meredith's voice sound disembodied from where she stood by the glass doors.

"What?" Ara gulped, the faint colour on her cheeks disappearing. "When? Who?"

"A man I met at a club several weeks back."

Ara huffed, hurt in her expressive eyes. "Why didn't you tell me you met a guy let alone a slayer? How do you even know he's a slayer?"

"Because first you were always at work and second, he saw us at Ladybower."

Ara paled.

"It's not your fault," Orelle answered Ara's unspoken statement, squeezing her hand.

"So he knows, we're dragons?"

Orelle shook her head. "We were able to leave right away, but I saw him as we did. I went to the bar where he works to tell him to piss off."

"You're supposed to kill him not just tell him to piss off." Ara scrunched her face.

That stopped Orelle from adding to what she wanted to say. She let out a lungful of air. "He knows where I live in town."

"Oh shit."

Orelle looked at Meredith whose mouth was pressed to a thin line.

"It's okay," she assured her Doyenne. "I've put

up my flat for sale."

"It's not that," Meredith replied, turning to them. "If he's tracked you down there, there's no reason why Havenshade will not be next."

Orelle agreed. "Which is why I've told him to meet me in Ladybower. We need to get the magi in to strengthen the shield around Havenshade."

Meredith nodded.

"Wait, what?" Ara sat up, unmindful of the blanket that covered her falling to the floor. "That's very close to where we are!"

"I know, but it will give me time to prepare." Orelle said.

"Prepare for what?"

Orelle and Meredith looked at each other.

"To kill my slayer."

* * *

Saxton sat on the edge of the bed, the rumpled sheet his only covering. His head hung between his hunched shoulders. He had the mother of all hangovers. His brain pounded within his cranium with even the faintest of breezes that accompanied any movement in the room. He gritted his teeth at the footsteps in the corridor before Sabine came in with a mug.

"Take this," she said softly. To Saxton she was as loud as a foghorn.

"What the fuck is that?" he growled.

"The smell of a bear with a thorn high up his ass."

"Owen?" Sabine smiled sweetly.

Owen grinned. "Yes, sweetheart?"

"Shut the fuck up."

Theo snorted a laugh but sobered under Sabine's go-on-I-dare-you glare. Sabine smoothed her features when she turned back to Saxton.

"Sax, This is going to help."

Saxton closed his eyes at the desolation sweeping through him. He wanted only one person to call him that way and she had disappeared. Again. The loss he felt didn't just stop at knowing she was gone. The gut feel he had when he and Braden had chased the car with the dragon inside haunted him. Now that he had Orelle's crumpled note in his hand, even a dumb schmuck could put two and two to make ten. There was no way Orelle could know he was a slayer unless she was the one in the car. An accessory to an age old feud.

"Drink."

Saxton scowled but did as Sabine ordered. Even his teeth became sensitive to the hot liquid, each movement, torture. The drink made him want to gag but Sabine held the bottom and tipped it causing some to trickle down the sides of his mouth.

"Jesus, Sabine. You don't have to drown him." Owen muttered.

"Drowning is reserved for you." She quipped. "Besides, you don't even know what it's like to drown."

"And you do." Owen mocked.

"Take your gripes outside." Theo pierced them

with a glare before he resumed Saxton's interrogation. "What will you do?"

The effects of Sabine's drink thankfully eased the pounding in his head and eliminated his hangover like a wet blanket being pulled away from him. Saxton sighed in gratitude. The sad thing about it? While Sabine's drink took out Thor's hammering, it didn't take out Loki crushing his heart with Orelle's betrayal.

Why would Orelle give up his dragon? Did she know he had to kill it to get his soul? The dragon he and Braden saw wasn't his. His dragon had a distinctive heartbeat only he could sense. Saxton would have felt his dragon nearby like a deep punch in the gut. The dragon he came upon in the reservoir didn't have either. A thought wormed its way into his mind. Could Orelle have decided to give up his dragon so that they could be together? The flicker of hope eased the ache of treachery but the heaviness was still there.

"Apollo?"

Saxton looked up at Theo.

"Go to where Orelle wants me to go and kill my dragon."

Theo's stony face relaxed. "I'll go with you. Owen can manage the bar."

"You're out of your bloody mind if you're going to make me baby sit the bar. Have Derrick or Braden do it." Owen's brows pulled low.

Saxton made his way to the bathroom, cupping water under the faucet to splash it on his face and around his neck.

"Fine." Theo's eyes glittered with amused irritation. "Tell Braden to come over. Derrick needs to stay in Pinehaven to track where the dragon will come from."

"Agreed." Saxton buttoned the waistband of his black denims then grabbed a long sleeved fitted cotton t-shirt from his chest of drawers. "The faster we find the lair, the faster we'll find our souls."

By the time Apollo, Jason, and Cadmus trekked to the woods overlooking the reservoir, thick flog had rolled in. Saxon hated it. It placed the slayers at a disadvantage despite their sharper senses. They'd had to bring torches and their weapons and that could alert the dragon of their presence.

"Dude, your chick's got guts asking you to meet her here." Owen, a.k.a. Cadmus mused then chuckled. "Are you sure this isn't a trap?"

"That's what I want to find out," Apollo said. He needed to hear Orelle admit that she was in the car that night.

"Cadmus is right," Jason said as they walked abreast. "Why here of all places?"

"I'll ask her when I see her." Apollo snapped before he exhaled.

"We're on your side, mate."

"Ignore me." He was antsy like when someone had an out of body experience and couldn't return to their body properly.

Something was wrong.

As soon as the thought took root in his mind, he

saw a dancing light several metres ahead.

"Over there." Cadmus pointed his axe.

"I see it." Saxton's eyes turned to slits. He inhaled sharply.

Orelle.

She arrived with an old lamp aloft casting an eerie glow over her. Saxton drew in another breath, unable to stop craving her tempting scent. She had changed her clothes. She wore a pair of slim fitting jeans tucked into knee high flat soled black boots and a white loose blouse. Her hair was curled and tumbled in dark waves around her shoulders. She was good enough to eat and tempt Saxton not to continue hunting for his dragon. But in the lamp's light, her face was a cool mask that hid whatever secrets she was privy to behind those dark eyes. Saxton's chest tightened when he caught the flicker of pain that flit through her eyes before it vanished.

"I should have known you'd bring back up," she said. Her voice wasn't how Saxton remembered. It was almost...dead.

"We'd still back him up even if he refused." Theo stepped forward and stabbed his sword to the ground with a thunk before leaning on it.

Orelle looked as though she was going to retort but exhaled instead. "I'd have done the same thing."

"What? Be the back-up?" Theo mocked.

"Why did you leave?" Apollo butted in, not liking the way Theo was treating Orelle. "Why the note?"

"How did you find out we were slayers?" Owen

got a question through.

Orelle laughed softly without humour. She shook her head before turning around to where she came from.

"I'll take you to your dragon." She flung the words at them as she walked.

"Orelle!"

Saxton ground his teeth when Orelle ignored him. Jaw tightening, he trudged ahead to keep pace with her.

"Goddammit, Orelle! What the hell's wrong with you?" He was annoyed that he had to raise his arm to protect himself from the low hanging branches while Orelle kept walking, her lamp aloft to light their way. Saxton was desperate and fuck that it showed. "The least you can do is tell me why you left after what's happened to us."

Orelle let out a laugh that was as bitter as it was sad. "There was never an us, Sax."

He stopped her, gripping her arm.

"Don't fuck with me."

A beatific smile curled on her lips. "I already did."

The air between them crackled enough to attract lightning. Saxton was at a loss. What happened to the girl who, a few days back, had unselfconsciously laughed in the rain? What happened to the woman who had shown so much passion when she came undone in his arms. Where was the woman who enjoyed eating as much as she enjoyed life? The person in front of him was an absolute stranger.

Saxton had an urge to rub the sudden ache in his chest that nearly robbed him of all thought. He let go of Orelle's arm slowly and watched her move away. Every step she took was a block of ice added to the wall locking down his emotions. He was stupid to think he could find happiness with someone he truly believed was the woman his destiny had found for him. He royally fucked up. Big time.

"You owe me an explanation. How did you know I was a slayer?"

* * *

It hurt the farther she stepped away from Saxton, the slayer Orelle now knew as Apollo. A slow burning rage filled her at the sight of their body armour. Dragon hide covered them from the shoulders down. Even the gauntlets they wore were made of the soft skin of some dead dragon's underbelly. It would keep them safe from the fire any dragon spewed, protecting them while they charged at the hapless creature with sharpened blades. It irritated her that she had been so short sighted not to think for a minute that Theo and Owen would allow Saxton to go on his own. She should have taken a page off the chronicles: Slayers came in pairs or trios even if only one had the bloody task of killing a dragon. They could maim a dragon up to an inch of its life but the coup de grace was done by the destined slayer. Orelle didn't know why there had to be an appointed slayer. All things considered it worked in their favour not to be killed. They had time to heal and then a time to kill.

"Orelle."

The sharpness of Saxton's voice drew her to a stop.

"Don't you know how?" She resumed her trek through the woods going deeper towards the clearing she had earlier prepared. If this wasn't a doom and gloom moment, she would have stopped and smelled the pines surrounding her. It's what her dragon would have loved. If things were different, she would have allowed her dragon to come out, unfurl her wings and take to the skies to be among the stars and maybe stay there for a time. To touch them and see if they moved and twinkled. Established science be damned. It didn't hold a candle to childlike wonder.

"It's so easy to answer my question, Orelle. Unless you have something to hide."

She didn't like the sneer in Saxton's voice or in any of the slayers. It was enough to spark her anger. "Since you're so hell bent on making a mockery of what I'm giving you, find your dragon yourself."

Saxton whirled her around.

"Don't touch me!"

"I want it to come from you."

"All right! I was the one in the car that drove off."

Saxton stiffened.

"That was me. In the reservoir," Orelle said, her voice soft but strong. "I was with the dragon that night."

Saxton let go of her arm and stepped away from

her. The way he looked at her …it was as if she had the plague. Disbelief was in the shake of his head, the truth he couldn't accept apparent in his eyes. Orelle was not sure which she preferred: being manhandled by Saxton just to have him near, or telling him not to touch her and long for his body when he moved away. Saxton's face was a mask of stone and a little piece of her heart crumbled. Even then he was magnificent, exuding power that she knew hid the man who pushed the right buttons to make her combust in his arms. Those few moments she shared with Saxton was like seeing the world in a brighter light. His smile made her melt, his laugh tickled her insides until the butterflies in her stomach flew in a frenzy. When Saxton took her, her body bowed in ecstasy and her blood sang in her veins. And when she fell back to earth, a sense of loss seeped into her bones when she and Saxton were no longer one. The truth of the matter was she couldn't get enough of Saxton Lance. She had fallen for him. He kept taking her breath away over and over again. Every time he did, the floating film that once encircled her heart wanted to break away and float to where it truly belonged.

Orelle's shoulders curled inward, her arms crisscrossing over her waist. "What did dragons ever do to you?"

"The reasons have been lost in time but I'm sure it's in the annals somewhere," Theo closed in. "Each slayer has a destined dragon called the Omega. And a destined dragon –"

176

"Holds a slayer's soul." Saxton finished.

Orelle looked at his flat cold eyes.

"All people have souls."

"We don't." Theo remarked. "It's the only thing that's stopping us from dying and finding peace."

"And vainglory." She muttered.

This time Theo grinned. "Exactly."

The puzzle started falling into place. Those moments when Saxton inhaled her every exhale, the times when she had felt both the agony of her heart tearing and the bliss of coming apart when Saxton was inside her. It was leading her to complete heartbreak.

"You've been given Dragonslayer 101," Saxton said before swinging his arm to point his axe at her. "Show us where the dragon is. I haven't got all day."

Orelle forced herself not to whimper. That moment when Saxton pointed the tip of his battle axe at her, she felt it. Felt the point as though it nicked her to draw blood. Her dragon roared but she stood her ground. It was getting more difficult to stop her dragon from taking over before they even reached the clearing. She wanted to rail at the sky and shatter the peaceful silence of the woods. Had she been in a Greek tragedy, she would have been writhing on the ground crying and wailing for Hades to take her. For all the riot inside her, her outward calm would have done Marcus Aurelius proud and would have earned her a place in the school of stoicism.

Orelle looked away. Gone was the man she cared for deeply. A dragonslayer had replaced him, determined to slay the very thing she was.

"This way." Every step she took brought her closer to the clearing.

And to her death.

CHAPTER EIGHTEEN

Saxton saw the stricken look Orelle tried to hide when she faced away from them. Or the pallor of her skin when Theo explained the reason for killing a dragon.

Was Orelle a dragon herself?

His mouth curled in disgust. The very reason he cut off ties with Perseus because of the road his friend decided to travel was the same path he was in danger of following. Perseus had lost everything – his home, his brethren, his reputation, yet gained so much more when he gave up his slayer's name to spend the rest of his life with his dragon.

He watched Orelle put one foot ahead of another and they hiked higher up the hill where the trees were starting to thin out. She looked as though she was already condemned even before she had been tried. Her scent, the one he always associated with her had become faint. If he could describe how sadness smelled like, it was this - the near absence of everything he loved about the woman walking in front of him. Orelle's dejection was palpable in the trudge of those legs that had been around his waist several hours ago as he plunged over and over again into her tight warmth. It was in the way the corners of her mouth curved downwards as though she had lost all reasons to smile. It was in the droop of those beautiful shoulders which he had been fortunate to caress with his mouth and the warmth of his breath. She looked up at the trees as if the branches that stood stock still had the solution that deviated from what had been fated for them.

Saxton's jaw tightened as he secured his axe behind his back once more. For Orelle's sake, he wished there was another solution too, but after he killed his dragon it was his duty to maim another. He had to be steadfast to do what he had been trained to do for centuries. With the way he felt for Orelle, it was going to be an uphill climb that was going to crush him inside. The pain that ripped across his torso blindsided him that he growled as he rubbed his hand across his chest.

"What's with the growl, Apollo?" Cadmus asked chuckling. "Can't wait to sink your axe into the dragon's neck, huh? I bet –"

The sound of wings flapping above them followed by the strong breeze stopped Cadmus from completing what he wanted to say. Everyone looked up. Through the fog, they could see a winged creature circling above them. It dove with a shrill cry, a plum of fire incinerating the treetops. The glow gave everyone a glimpse of an iridescent red dragon with burning red eyes. Its jaws were wide open, its teeth menacing almost glowing against its fiery breath. Orelle and the dragonslayers dove for cover before it landed, crushing tree trunks in some improbable scorched earth activity in the north of England. The

180

lamp and torches were forgotten in the wake of the blaze that glowed around them.

The slayers stood, all in battle mode while the dragon waited. It's tail flicked behind it, a tail tapering into something similar to a stingray's. It hit a pine tree as though its mere presence was distasteful. The bark split diagonally like a hot knife to butter. Save for the solitary horn in the middle of the dragon's head and its wide webbed wings that were currently folded against its body, the dragon didn't have any horns scaling its back or anywhere else in its body. Instead its red scales glimmered in the eerie fog laden glow of the fire from the trees. It shifted to a darker orange hue, and of all colours, pink. What it didn't have in deadly horns, it had the power to mesmerise the slayers in spades. All three slayers stared at it agog.

"Seriously, pink?" Cadmus voiced his disbelief breaking the dragon's thrall.

Angered, the dragon huffed and screeched. It directed its fiery breath at Cadmus before surging back to the skies. Theo stretched back, ready to catapult his sword like a spear.

"No, Jason." Cadmus growled. "That's my Omega. It's mine. See you both back in Pinehaven!" He ran down the slope cutting and bellowing his way through whatever impeded his chase.

"At least that dragon had the sense not to burn the whole forest down." Jason commented. "May have felled trees but didn't start a fire."

They looked around. The fallen trunks were

blackened in places, crushed in others. The damp ground stopped the leaves from turning to kindling and the slayers stomped on the stray embers they saw.

"Okay," Saxton turned to where Orelle stood. "I'm sure you –"

She was gone.

He swore.

"Guess she had back-up after all." Theo drawled resting the flat of his blade on his shoulder.

"Back off, Theo."

"Sax, what's wrong with you? She's just a girl you fucked. Too bad she's a dragon –" Theo didn't get another word out. Saxton landed a right hook on his jaw causing him friend to stagger back.

"What the fuck, man! Has she addled your cock too much you've become the pussy?" Theo thundered, wiping the blood from his split lip.

Saxton's fist uncurled, the skin on his knuckles stinging. He despised it when Theo had the gall to describe Orelle as though she was some whore who had other men share her bed. The very idea made him see red.

"Let's move out," he said, his voice cold. Saxton never apologised. Saying something after a heated exchange was more than enough made up for it. His ego couldn't bear the word 'sorry'.

They trudged upwards depending on Saxton's tracking of Orelle's scent.

"Stop."

Saxton continued.

"Apollo, stop!"

"Now what the hell for?" he grounded turning around to face Theo. The moon was almost on top of them casting a pale glow over the area.

"Can you hear that?"

"Hear what?"

Theo's puzzled look gave way to wonder. "That voice. It's beautiful."

Saxton snorted as he resumed scaling the slope. "Since when? Since you heard yourself speak?"

"I can't believe you can't hear it!"

"I don't hear a damn thing." Saxton exhaled in annoyance. "Are you coming or going?"

Theo had a bewildered look. "I need to find out where that voice is coming from. Sorry mate, need to bail. Sure you can handle your dragon without pissing your pants?"

"Next time it won't be my fist hitting your jaw, Jason. It'll be my axe."

Theo snorted. "See you back in Pinehaven. Hopefully in one piece."

* * *

There was no point in Orelle staying with the slayers. She could have ran away and let them search for her. But Meredith and Ara's safety trumped her instinct to flee. When Orelle left Havenshade amid Ara's tears, Meredith had called in several of the dragon magi to reinforce the spells around the lair to avoid detection. Every quarter, the magi went around the country buttressing the lairs with magick. Since

Havenshade was due for a visit, no one suspected what Meredith, Orelle, and Ara were trying to hide. Having two incidents of possible slayer incursions in near succession wouldn't bode well for them. The Gathering would only see it as a sign of weakness and incompetence. Meredith could be stripped of the Doyenne's mantle and be given to someone else. Havenshade might just be given a real dragon lady. Orelle could only imagine the disappointment of Meredith's family. It was why she had to succeed in consciously luring Saxton and killing him this time.

The air in the clearing was crisp, the fog bank left behind in the lower part of the slope. Orelle heard the undergrowth crunch under someone's footsteps. She turned, surprised to see only Saxton coming up the incline.

"I didn't know slayers liked playing chicken." She mocked and she felt a small sense of triumph when Saxton narrowed his eyes. A reaction. That's something.

"Was the other dragon a ploy?"

"I've never seen that dragon before." Orelle shook her head. It was the truth. The dragon was as beautiful as it was tragic. Its red colour reminded Orelle of those really blood red lipsticks film noir actresses used or the pigeon's blood rubies they wore. While all dragons of their kind had horns on their backs, the red dragon had none save for the solitary one in the middle of its head. A dragon was as good as its horns so one without the requisite number of protrusions was not considered a dragon at all, but an aberration.

"I don't believe you."

Saxton's cold voice drew her away from her musings.

"Think what you like." Orelle expelled a breath.

He looked away, his jaw hard.

"I didn't want to believe that it could be you at the reservoirs. I thought I was imagining your scent because we had only just seen each other that afternoon."

"What scent are you talking about?" Orelle frowned. "I don't wear perfume."

He glared at her. "It's what brought me to you at the club. All this time you've been using it to lure me to you."

"What?" Orelle looked at him, aghast. A laugh of disbelief bubbled out of her. "I didn't even know you before then." She walked away from him still shaking her head. "I didn't realise what an arrogant conceited bastard you turned out to be. A slayer's glowing attribute."

"And yet you came to my bed."

Her face grew hot. "By mutual consent. You came to me, remember?"

"I came inside you, Orelle. Let's get the facts straight."

She laughed in incredulity. "You're bringing that up now? Why?"

"Because I can't understand how a woman like you could get embroiled in this bloody business with dragons."

Orelle felt her brows rise so high, her eyelids stretched upward.

"A woman like me? Be careful what you say next, slayer."

"A woman I'd have given up killing my dragon if it meant that I'd have you with me for as long as you'll have me."

She inhaled sharply. Pivoting she moved away as her eyes began to smart. *No*. She wasn't going to give in to crying or look for hope in Saxton's words when there was none.

"Nothing too serious happened between us other than fucking each other's brains out, Saxton."

"It was more than sex, Orelle. Don't lie to yourself."

"And you would know?"

"What have the dragons done to deserve your loyalty?"

Saxton's sudden change of the subject was giving her a mental whiplash.

"Because they never harmed anyone!" Her dragon was restless and her limbs were becoming icy, a precursor to her changing.

"Dragons took over where dinosaurs left of." Saxton's voice carried through the edge of the clearing as crisp as the air around them. "Some witch decided to play tricks and made dragons the keepers of slayers' souls."

"It wasn't a witch. It was a warlock who formed the first group of slayers."

Saxton's eyes narrowed. "How would you know

that?"

"It's written in the dragon chronicles." Her feet were like ice now and her heart was growing inside her chest.

"I ask again, what have they done to deserve your loyalty and how the hell do you know so much about dragons?" Saxton's bellow could make a grown man piss in his pants. But Orelle was past caring. Her dragon had broken the chains of sanity Orelle had manacled it to and she was too weak to fight it. Her heartbeat raced so fast. Her limbs went beyond icy cold to burning all at once. She felt her pupils changing shape and saw her mortal self, withdraw into her mind, relinquishing her hold on her body to allow her beast take her place.

"Because I am one, Saxton. And I am your dragon."

CHAPTER NINETEEN

Saxton thought he didn't hear right. His scowl seemed permanently etched on his face. But when Orelle raised her arms as though to worship the moon and started to grow, he staggered back as chills raced down his spine. Out of reflex, his hand gripped the handle of his axe and pulled it out of its harness at his back. He crouched and bellowed, but the sound was more of a man tormented than someone victorious. The whole time they exchanged barbs about dragons, his suspicions about Orelle before shoving them to the back of his mind did not prepare him for the truth morphing in front of him. Orelle's mournful cry rent the air before it shifted to a piercing shriek that made the fine hairs on his arms and on the nape of his neck stand. She stretched high above him, her skin becoming mottled and transforming to scales of burnished gold like the rays of the setting sun. It shimmered and glistened when she moved with fluid grace reminding Saxton of the full moon's reflection that rippled on the surface of an ocean. Her spine lengthened beyond her feet to form her tail that swished as she turned around to face him. Twenty feet of deadly force that slashed and felled trees unfortunate enough to stay in its path. Horns dotted halfway down his Omega's back. Orelle twisted her long neck to blow her sulphuric breath away from him and Saxton ached. Oh God, how his heart ached. Even in her dragon form, Orelle refused to harm him when she could have easily swiped him with one of her powerful legs where her deadliest weapons were. Fine razor sharp protrusions that retracted from underneath her scales used to impale any unsuspecting adversary.

An angry growl rose from deep within Saxton, a harsh denial punching its way out of his throat. His grip on his axe slackened and the spear tip thunked into the moist earth. All thought nearly fled save for the churning of his gut as his senses became attuned to the presence of his soul that beat strong and steady within his prized Omega.

Who was also now his beautiful curse.

His heart and mind pulled at each other as his eyes beheld the truth. The scent no one else could smell, the attachment to the spilled blood on the tree trunk, the sadness that nearly unmanned him replacing the jubilation when his axe nearly found its mark. All those signs pointed to the one person he wanted to have for his own.

Orelle.

A roar punctuated the stillness of the valley like the rolling thunder that came after the crack of lightning. Dimly Saxton realised it didn't come from Orelle.

It came from him.

His head bowed dejectedly between his shoulders. He stared unseeingly at his axe's blade, a stark dull greyish white in the moonlight. He willed his hand to grasp the handle but his brain refused to follow his command.

So this was how desolation felt. The loss of the will to live. Like a mental scrapbook, he saw moments with Orelle – his private dancer with a voracious appetite and an infectious laugh. A woman with a beatific smile who enjoyed simple things, like the splash of the rain on her face in a squall. She was his passion, his fulfilment. She was his full stop after the longest sentence of being alone. His body remembered her screams of ecstasy that brought him hurtling towards his own completion. She was the woman he knew he couldn't live without.

But the dragon who had to die so he could redeem his soul.

How could he kill her now that he knew he loved her?

"You have to go." His voice was tight with emotion, his tone drowned by the sudden rustling of the trees as Orelle flapped her wings gently. "Didn't you hear me? Go!"

Orelle's vertical amber eyes watched him before she moved her head.

Did she just say no?

"Bloody hell, woman! This is not a game!"

Orelle moved her head once more and Saxton saw her in her human form, flicking her hair away from her shoulder. He nearly gawked, incredulous at her insouciance.

Damn if he didn't find that attractive.

190

"You will die!"

A sword whizzed past Saxton's ear and lodged itself straight in the middle of Orelle's chest. She reared with a screech of agony, her blood gushing from the sides of the blade. Saxton whirled around, fury making him grab his axe and crouch with a snarl.

Theo came running from the trees, his other sword in his hand.

"What the fuck are you playing at, Apollo?" he shouted, his face harsh and cruel in the firelight. "I'm game if you want to play with your dragon first."

The clink of something like armour sounded behind Saxton. Orelle's eyes were blood red and filled with rage. The deadly projections she had on her legs were in full display. She advanced like a cobra, taking a swipe at Theo. Theo was quicker, rolling away with only seconds to spare before Orelle could impale his head against her leg..

"She's mine, Jason." Saxton bellowed. "I will kill my Omega when I'm fit and ready."

Theo cackled as he stood. "You fucked her man! If you had any decency left at all, you should have killed her the moment she changed."

Saxton's chest expanded. Jason was right. It was what they were trained to do.

God, how he hated his friend right now.

"You think I didn't hear?" Theo sneered. "You'll thank me one day knowing I helped you take her down. Living in the fringes of our society with your name removed from the chronicles isn't the right way to go. You said that when you told us about Perseus."

Saxton's jaw clenched so hard he thought he'd break it. There was no way he could deny that at a time when he didn't understand.

The roar of the living furnace behind him intensified. Saxton's back heated. The dragon hide of his armour shielded him but still singed part of his hair on the back of his head. The acrid smoke of burning human hair mixed with the scent of burning wood. A ring of fire kept them inside the clearing as Orelle's breath hit some kindling.

Another thwack sounded before Orelle screamed again in agony.

"Jason! Stop!" Saxton pushed Theo hard but not enough to topple him.

"I'm giving you your soul, Apollo! And you've become a coward because of some bitch!"

"With my axe?" Saxton smashed his fist against Theo's jaw. Theo turned back to face him and grinned, his own blood coating some of his teeth.

"Knowing how much you love your weapons, that's the only way you'll get your axe back. You're a dragonslayer for fuck's sake. Act like one!"

Orelle twisted her head from side to side before unfurling her wings. She bent her legs to take flight. Her claws hadn't even left the ground when she shrieked once more falling back. Her wing curled by her side, bloodied and torn as Theo's other sword sliced through.

"No!"

Theo stormed at Orelle, viciously unsheathing

the sword embedded on her chest before Saxton could tackle him to the ground. He was able to punch Theo once before he got kicked away.

Pain, agony the likes of no other nearly made Saxton vomit. It seared his chest and his back as if he too had been stabbed. Orelle fell to her side, the impact sending a strong sulphuric wind across the clearing, causing leaves and brittle branches to rustle and break. Her eyes rolled in their sockets, the light in them starting to dim. Her nostrils that had flared once every five seconds now became once in two. Theo pointed his sword, soaked in Orelle's golden blood, at Saxton. Blood that hissed the moment it hit the ground.

"Your turn."

Saxton narrowed his eyes at Theo in fury. Dust and sweat covered them both now. They were no longer Saxton Lance and Theo Rennick. They were the Dragonslayers Apollo and Jason.

Apollo staggered to his feet at the same time taking his remaining axe from behind his back. He roared and launched at Jason, all his rage and anguish in his strike. But Jason anticipated his move lifting his sword to deflect the blow. Metal sparked against metal. Apollo's arm arced wide before his weapon clanged once more against Jason's blade. Air whooshed out of Apollo when Jason's fist rammed into his solar plexus and grunted in pain when Jason's blade sliced his cheek. Warm blood gushed out of the cut but Apollo was beyond caring. Orelle was hurt because he didn't expect Jason to return. He needed to make it up to Orelle. Needed to ease the torment his Omega was going through.

Because of his failure to protect her.

Apollo pushed Jason before turning in a semi-circle to slam the pommel of his axe against the side of Jason's head. Jason staggered, dazed as the blow broke his skin and blood flowed from the cut. Apollo hollered his anguish striking the slayer he had called brother for hurting the woman he loved. Right now, the shame brought by his inability to fulfil his destiny was nothing compared to the grief he'd feel if he lost Orelle.

Jason continued to deftly parry Apollo's blows. Before Apollo could strike him once more, they heard terrifying cries and looked up to see two dragons circling lower and lower in a helix formation before they landed, flanking Orelle. One was the red dragon they had seen earlier, and the other was a dragon Apollo didn't expect to see again. Its silvery blue mane was unmistakable since the last time he saw it after it dove to the depths of the sea, bringing with it the slayer...

Who now slid down its back.

The silver blue dragon's chest expanded, roaring as it let out a mouthful of blue white flame. The heat was so intense that Apollo had to back almost ten feet away. However, the dragon wasn't focused on him. It was intent on Jason, chasing him away from the clearing. Jason backed away, unable to withstand the heat.

"Come back, Saxton!" he shouted. "Or I swear to

God, I will hunt you and your dragon down!" His face was a mask of anger and betrayal before he ran away to concede the round.

The former dragonslayer strode towards Saxton, hands raised.

"I'm not here to fight you," Perseus stated.

Saxton didn't dally. "Save the brawl for another time." He sidestepped Perseus and ran to Orelle. The wary and dangerous amber eyes of the two dragons watched him. Their growls were joined by their sulphuric breaths that would have melted the lungs of an ordinary mortal. Saxton didn't give a shit. There was no reason for him to continue if Orelle left him. The dragons could have his sorry carcass after he tended to Orelle.

Her golden blood gushed in a stream from the wound inflicted by Theo's sword. Saxton's axe was still embedded by her shoulder.

"Take it out and you can have your soul right where you stand." Perseus voice was terse. "Is that what you want?"

Saxton stared at a barely breathing Orelle. His hand swiped at his face belatedly realizing the wound Theo had inflicted. "Will your dragons allow me to do that?"

Low growls came from the dragons' throats, their sharp teeth bared in a snarl, their eyes changing back to red.

"I will tell them not to interfere," Perseus said. "And not to kill you. Your Omega is dying, Apollo. Decide quickly."

Saxton looked into Orelle's eyes. In her dragon form her head was just as tall as Saxton. Orelle blinked slowly. In his heart, he heard her.

It's not your fault, slayer. This was meant to be. Your soul floats inside me and waits for you to claim it. I return it to you willingly.

Saxton turned to Perseus and he couldn't hide his anguish.

"Help her, Ty. Help me. Please don't let Orelle die."

CHAPTER TWENTY

Saxton stood at the pier watching the bustle of activity. The water's cerulean colour appeared to mirror the sky's hue overhead. The sun twinkled in the ripples of the tiny waves as boats arrived with their catch of Neptune's treasures. A strong breeze whipped the sails of the boats to bring them homeward bound. It tousled Saxton's hair and flattened the clothes on his body.

The same clothes he wore since Orelle bled to an inch of her life three days ago. He couldn't let go of his soiled wear not only because her blood caked parts of it but also because her sweet meadow scent remained with it. It was as though by wearing her blood close to his skin, Saxton could keep whatever connection they still had with each other.

His musings were cut short by the sharp and boisterous laughter of some of the fishermen. Full bodied, it was filled with joy and they were welcomed by people of this tucked away cove by the North Sea. Greenisle was buffered from the rest of humanity by a huge mountain thickly covered with tall trees whose tips reached endlessly to the sky. Behind Saxton, pastel walled and white washed houses dotted the mountainside in descending order. To his far left was the rest of the city with skyscrapers that shimmered in the sunlight – the business and shopping district. Overhead dragons flew freely circling the azure sky in dazzling shimmering colours of jewels.

Precious stones for precious creatures.

It was a beautiful day and Saxton had received his soul.

But he couldn't care less for what good was it when its guardian was flitting between life and death?

He faced the wind resolutely. His arms were not crossed in relaxation over his chest. It was more like his hands clutched his biceps as though bracing himself for the inevitable fate he refused to accept.

Footsteps approached him from behind.

"Apollo."

He inclined his head to the side to acknowledge his visitor before resuming his steady gaze at the horizon. Perseus drew to stand by his side and neither spoke for a time.

"Once I thought I'd prefer being called by that name rather than my own." Saxton's voice carried across the wind.

"It's still yours."

"As your slayer's name is yours, Ty. Yet you refused to be called by that name."

Ty smiled. "Touché. It was who we were, Sax. Something we can never erase."

"It's a bloody symbol of our sins if you ask me."

They remained silent. While Saxton marvelled at how Greenisle was able to merge the old with the new, he couldn't find joy in its beauty or the majesty of the dragons that coasted the winds above them.

Ty nodded. "It will fade in time."

"What will?" Saxton glanced at his long lost friend. "The name?"

"No," Ty said quietly. "The guilt."

Saxton exhaled and whatever resolve he had to remain strong dissolved in the sudden mist that coated his eyes.

"I can't lose her, Ty. She said it had to be done."

"There was no point in keeping your soul within Orelle. It was holding on by a thin thread," Ty said. "If it broke away and entered her veins that really would have killed her."

Saxton let out a bitter chuckle. "The worst ever Catch 22 I've heard in my godforsaken life."

"Orelle is strong. Lia said so. She'll push through," Ty said on a breath. He smoothed his hair over his head, like it would stop the wind from ruffling it once more.

"I saw you sink your axes into Lia all those centuries ago." Saxon began. "Were you able to recover your soul?"

Ty's sharp features softened with the pain of remembrance. He nodded. "But not like this. My soul was still intact inside her. It was easier for the magi to transfer it to me."

"Ty."

The softest voice Saxton ever heard carried across the breeze like a happy sigh. The two former slayers turned and beheld a woman of beauty with silvery blue hair and the deepest amethyst eyes. She looked at Saxton with a wealth of wisdom and acceptance.

"Orelle's waking." She wrinkled her nose. "You better change though. You don't want her dragon smelling its blood on you."

Saxton looked down then back at Lia. He felt his cheeks burn, his arms hanging by his sides. He swallowed but his throat seemed to have thickened.

"Lia...I'm..." He couldn't say the words because of the shame he felt.

Lia smiled and approached him. She squeezed his arm.

"I forgive you, slayer," she said softly. "Now make yourself presentable. Your Omega is waiting."

* * *

Orelle didn't think that surfacing from water could be so painful. Geez, she must swim more often. Maybe get a few pointers from Ara. But even as she broke water, her chest still hurt as if her lungs couldn't pull in the air she needed...

...to breathe.

The clearing, the changing, Theo...

Saxton.

Her world she knew rushed in and with it came a more intense pain. Fear. Rage. Orelle pulled in a harsh breath unmindful of the pain that merrily wound its way through her veins, goading her to succumb to eternal oblivion. The hell she would. She'd get her answers first before she would even

200

negotiate with Death.

With painstaking clarity, she did a body scan. She knew she was no longer in her dragon form and saw her dragon curled, asleep.

In pacem.

A huge reptilian eye opened, the black slit in the centre of a pool of amber, watched her. It held no rancour but no sympathy either. It was just what it was. And as her beast closed its eye to sleep, it let out a thought into Orelle's mind.

It's okay.

She shifted and winced. Her shoulder was sore, so was the middle of her chest. She vaguely recalled the moment Theo threw his sword, Saxton's axe, and then another sword at her. Orelle thought her windpipe would collapse and all she wanted to do was fly away to Havenshade to heal and disappear for good. She moved her right arm. Yup, she wasn't going to be writing with her right hand anytime soon.

Where was she? She inhaled the sea in the air. A gentle breeze cooled her face. In the distance, she heard the waves slapping against the shore and cheerful voices.

And the wings of a dozen dragons flying freely.

Where was Saxton? Did he leave with Theo? Sadness was a thief taking her heart from her. Saxton had looked down at her with eyes filled with regret when she thought she was in the last throes of her life. She scanned inward…yes, the film was gone.

Saxton had finally taken his soul.

How she survived was something Orelle vowed

she'd find out later.

A heavy weight lay on her chest as if her dragon sat on her. That very moment, Orelle promised herself that once the heartbreak became a dull throb, she'd move on. To live to tell the tale about how she survived after bequeathing a slayer's soul back...that was a first.

"Orelle..."

She didn't recognise the voice. She took another wincing breath and slowly released the air. It eased the physical pain centred in her sternum.

Much better.

"It's time you woke up. Don't you think?"

No, she thought stubbornly. She still wanted to go to sleep. It was the only way she could heal both her body and her heart.

She heard a slow and resigned sigh.

"Let me." There was a shuffle as though people were changing places.

"I'll come back later." She heard the female voice say.

Orelle's sluggish pulse beat deeper. Could it be? Her heart suddenly flipped when strong firm hands covered her own.

"Orelle, please baby. Open your eyes."

Baby?

Her eyes rolled inside her lids in an attempt to pry them open but they remained shut. Why did it have to take every ounce of her strength to open them and see where she was? She tried again. Finally!

She blinked several times. Everything was hazy

as though she was looking through thick mullioned windows that had swirls in the centre of the panes. After several attempts to moisten her eyes, she saw everything around her. But nothing prepared her for the face that filled her vision.

"Sax…ton?"

The sides of his eyes crinkled. His smile was one of relief.

"Hey."

She closed her eyes again, afraid that she was dreaming. After everything that happened, why would he still be with her? She opened her eyelids once more.

He was still there, filling the space in front of her.

She swallowed the emotion threatening to burst out of her. She looked away at the billowing veils that allowed the sea breeze in from the huge doorway. They looked like fine mist catching prisms from the sun. The cream walls of her room were bare save for an alcove with a statue inside it. The room reminded Orelle of the houses in Santorini and Tolkien's Middle Earth.

Her eyes found Saxton once more as she inhaled the scent of roses and jasmine from the huge flower vase in one corner of the room.

"What…happened to your face?"

Saxton touched the deep gash below his cheekbone. His mouth quirked.

"A remembrance of what I used to be."

Her brow furrowed. "I don't understand. If

you're here then I must be your prisoner." She looked around again unmindful of her discomfort. "Am I a prisoner to be feted before being tortured by other slayers?"

"Bloody hell, they must really have given you enough medicine to warp your brain." Saxton muttered, his smile deteriorating slowly to bemusement.

"Slayer!"

A pulse ticked on Saxton's jaw. "I'm not a slayer any more. And no one will hurt you. They'll have to go through me first before they touch you."

She exhaled the breath she held. "You…you're just saying that. You're going to torture me because I didn't die when you took your soul. I don't feel it, Sax. I no longer feel your soul inside me." Resignation joined her breath. Shit. She hoped Saxton didn't flay her too long before he allowed her to die. She could only take so much from him.

Because the moment Saxton's soul was removed for her was the moment she also let go of her heart.

"Are you this nonsensical when you're healing?" Exasperated amusement laced his question.

"Are you this quiet when contemplating harm?" Orelle countered. "Maybe you can write a book, How to Torture a Dragon."

Saxton leaned back on the wooden chair with a noisy sigh. He shook his head. "Where the hell did you even get the idea of me hurting you?"

"Because you're a slayer and I don't know where I am." Her voice rose in hysteria.

Before she could utter another word, Saxton leaned over and captured her mouth in a kiss that took her breath away. She whimpered and writhed on the bed, aching to be closer to him. Only Saxton had the power to do this to her. Need flowed like lava as her pulse raced in desire than panic. An ache that only Saxton could assuage bloomed in the centre of her sex and she had to press her thighs together to try to ease her lust. Yet at the back of her mind, she knew that Saxton's lips on hers and the heat that radiated from his body were only temporary. Eons of enmity between slayer and dragon made it impossible for her to be his. Finally he pulled away to gaze at her, his fingers tucking the stray strands of her hair behind her ear.

"I'm no longer a slayer, Orelle." His voice was hoarse. "That's what I've been trying to tell you. Hear and accept that truth. And no one will condemn us here in Greenisle."

"I can smell my sulphuric breath and you still kiss me…wait…what?" In her shock, she pushed her palm against Saxton's chest and gave a guttural shout when the wound on her shoulder pulled harshly against the surrounding skin. "Damn it, Sax. I need an explanation before we become horny."

A deep chuckle that rumbled up his chest matched the laughter in his eyes. A shaft of electricity skittered down Orelle's spine when his look became filled with promises of sensually decadent nights.

"Hmmm….I smell your pussy's sweetness,

205

Orelle. It's making me hungry and thirsty. I don't mind hiding inside your blankets while you heal. As long as you have your legs spread wide, so my fingers and tongue can play with you."

"Saxton," she groaned unable to stop her body's response when he grazed his mouth against her ear before dipping to gently suck the pulse at the base of her neck. "Please, I need to know what's happened."

"Ahh good, Orelle. You're awake."

Orelle nearly squeaked at the intrusion, embarrassment reddening her face. She peered over Saxton's shoulder as her eyes followed the woman who entered the room. The woman's silvery blue hair which had darker blue strands flowed like a smooth curtain down to her waist. She had the most unusual eyes. Lavender to almost dark blue. She wore a loose white blouse and powder blue linen trousers. Orelle's eyes widened in stupefaction.

Dragon.

"Yes, I am." Her visitor beamed. "I'm Lia. How are you feeling?"

Orelle could only stare at her, speechless. "Uh…fine. Feeling better than when…you pulled me out of the clearing."

Lia nodded. "I did. I had help."

"The red dragon," Orelle said. "Thank you for saving my life. Where is the red one? I'd like to thank her too."

Lia's smile faltered. "She isn't here."

Orelle's forehead creased. "Why?"

"Because she says it's not her time yet, but I'm

sure she knows of your gratitude."

"Hold up." Orelle raised her hand and grimaced at the sight of more bandages. "From the start please."

"You're in Greenisle." Lia explained. "It's my home and a place where the enmity between dragon and slayer doesn't exist."

"Excuse me?" Orelle let out a shaky laugh. "You're kidding right?"

"And yet here you are with your slayer." Lia stated softly. "You know that Saxton can maim me before my destined slayer gives me the coup de grace. But he's right here within striking distance and still doesn't do anything to harm me."

"If he did, I'd kill him." A wry voice came from the doorway. "Besides why will he do that when he knows you are the love that was missing in my life? He understands that now."

A man just as handsome and as muscular as Saxton sauntered into the room. His wavy dark hair was cut short and he had the most arresting blue eyes Orelle had ever encountered in her life.

"I'm Ty formerly known as Perseus. You've met Lia, my Omega. She was the one who told me to risk Saxton's anger and see him at the bar."

"Why?" Orelle asked suddenly self-conscious at how she looked.

"Lia has the gift of sight. She saw you and Saxton together but also saw danger lurking." Ty turned to Saxton. "Even after I left the bar that day, we have been keeping tabs on you both. Thank God we did."

"Ty, you've got any opticians here?" Saxton broke in casually.

Ty's brow slightly puckered. "Yeah. Why? Need some glasses, old man?"

"No, you do. And get the darkest sunglasses." Saxton snapped. "Orelle can't take her eyes of your ancient blues."

Ty's shoulders shook before it became a full blown laugh. "C'mon Lia, let's leave the horny kids alone."

Saxton growled. Ty rolled his eyes before training them once more at Orelle.

"Believe what my Omega told you," Ty said. "You are both safe here."

When they left, Orelle turned to Saxton. There was a new emotion in his eyes that made her heart skip a beat.

"Sax?"

Saxton left the bed and knelt beside it. He held her hand and kissed it. Orelle waited with bated breath for a time that seemed like an eternity.

"I'm sorry."

Just like that the dam burst inside and the reservoir of emotions she held in check flowed down the side of her face. She pulled in a breath, her face scrunching through the pain in her chest before letting out sobs that wracked her body. The bed creaked under Saxton's weight once more before he pulled her into his arms. He helped her curl into him mindful of her injuries. But the stabbing sensation that caused her body to protest was nothing compared to Saxton's body beside her. It felt better than any healing balm because it cemented the fissures that had appeared in her heart and her own soul.

She couldn't live without him, she knew that. It didn't matter that her heart had ceased to be his soul's prison. Her heart would not beat if Saxton left. It would only beat in order to exist until such time when Death decided to take pity on her.

"Shh...Orelle...babe."

"I can't live without you." She hiccupped. "If you're going to say goodbye, please lie. Don't say goodbye yet." She looked up at him, tears streaming. "Stay with me and let me heal. Then when I have gone to sleep, walk out the door as though you're going somewhere. At least I'll keep on thinking that you're just outside but not gone for good."

"Orelle..." Saxton's voice was pained. A fresh flood of tears fell in torrents drenching his shirt.

"Please, that's all I ask."

Saxton let her cry, holding her close. Orelle pulled whatever strength his body gave her, absorbing as much of him as she could to coat her veins and heart with his own smell. She felt like an ant hoarding for the long winter. But hers wasn't just a long winter. Hers was losing Saxton forever.

And for the second time since Saxton's soul peeled away, her heart broke.

CHAPTER TWENTY ONE

The only sound filtering through the room the moment Orelle's sobs ceased was that of sea and surf. Even though her nose was clogged, she could still smell the salt in the breeze. Orelle closed her eyes listening to Saxton's beating heart under her ear.

"That day at the bar," she began, staring blankly at the wall. "I wanted to flay you alive."

Saxton shifted beside her. "Why?"

"Because you invaded my privacy."

His chest expanded then deflated. "I couldn't help it."

"Why?"

"Because," he shifted so that they could look at each other. "I needed you. I couldn't let another minute pass that you weren't with me."

Orelle's eyes widened. She searched his face and her heart squeezed at the anguish she saw in his eyes.

"When Jason…" he gritted. "Theo threw his sword, I knew it was the right thing to do. But how could something I believed to be right feel so wrong?"

She blinked. Tears continued to trickle like a brook down the side of her face.

"You know why it felt so wrong?" Saxton asked.

She shook her head, sniffing through her clogged

210

nose.

"Because I had fallen for you."

"Oh Sax."

He kissed her. A soft and sweet kiss filled with hope. "I fell for you Orelle, that's why I was searching for you. In such a short time, in a world where sex is so easy, you meant more to me than that. It didn't feel right that you weren't with me. I was desperate to find you and when I realised you were my Omega." His breath fanned her face as he closed his eyes. "I never knew."

"And you accused me of luring you," she chided. "That was bang out of–"

She made a soft sound with her sigh under the onslaught of Saxton's kiss. The bedsheets rustled when she attempted to pillow her head once more on Saxton's chest.

"Sax," she said against his mouth. "I can't breathe. My nose is clogged."

Saxton's shoulders shook before his mouth moved against her jaw before trailing his lips down the column of her throat to the base of her neck.

"How did Ty and Lia know when to arrive?" Orelle asked after a long while.

"I haven't got a clue." Saxton admitted. "Theo and I were in the middle of killing each other when they did. Lia breathed her fire at Theo before Ty told me to join him so they could get you to the magi. You were bleeding like crazy. Bloody hell, Orelle. I've never been so scared in my entire existence at the thought of losing you."

Saxton held her so tightly she squirmed causing him to laugh softly.

"I don't remember anything after the clearing," she admitted. Try as she might her memory remained hazy.

"Lia and the other dragon held you in their claws until we got here."

"And my blood?"

"We were too high for your blood to do any damage below." Saxton answered. "At the very least people might think Tinkerbell went bat-shit crazy and sprinkled pixie dust after drinking with the lost boys."

Orelle's mouth quivered in a grin before she sobered. "And your soul? How did you take it out without killing me?"

"I told the magi that if you didn't survive, I'd kill them."

"You what? Ow!" she gasped then hissed at the pain angrily spreading through her body. "Shit, Sax. You don't threaten the magi. At. All."

"I'm a dragonslayer. So sue me." He snorted. "They didn't hex me or do all sorts of things they would normally do to someone like me. When they saw how bad you were they worked on you immediately. At first, they were afraid you wouldn't make it. But you're strong. While Lia and the rest of the dragons held most of your pain at bay with their combined fire, the magi were able to lift my soul from your body to put it inside mine."

Orelle played with a stray thread on Saxton's

homespun shirt.

"I guess this means that you'll be going back to the Brew Bar now that you have your soul back."

"I am not leaving you, woman. Theo is too furious with me to have my head or report me to the Convenors that I fell for my Omega. That was what I did to Ty and I am going to regret that for the rest of my life." Saxton sighed shaking his head. He looked down at her, his grey green eyes holding her captive. "Unless you want me to?"

A ray of happiness filtered through her but Orelle quashed it.

"But you'll be condemned."

"Better a condemned man loving you for the rest of my life than a victorious slayer whose life has no meaning save for the praise of his peers. Hell, I don't even want to be an elder."

Finally Orelle smiled, really smiled. Her mouth widened, her lips curving upwards. Her heart sang and her soul rejoiced. Even her dragon purred inside her. When she was well enough, she would find a way to contact Meredith. Sadness weighed as heavy as an anvil on her chest knowing she would never see her sisters again. But there was hope. She could feel it down to the very marrow of her bones. And someday, she knew she'd be reunited with Ara and Meredith. Until that time came, she'd enjoy every moment she had with Saxton. She'd get her strength from him to weather whatever challenges lay ahead for both of them.

"Saxton?"

"Hmm…?" he looked down at her.

Her arm went around his neck bringing his mouth closer to hers.

"I love you too."

EPIL⊙GUE

Theo surveyed the destruction in the clearing from a safe distance with narrowed eyes. Television stations around the country and even some from across the pond and the continent showed live feeds of the devastation that charred several trees and blackened part of Hope Valley. The police were looking for an arsonist and appealing for information from anyone who may have witnessed the carnage. Quasi-experts and crackpots attributed it to a possible alien landing gone awry because of a crop circle within a friggin' forest.

Saxton didn't come home. His disappearance cast a black mark on all of them. In fact, the slayers of Pinehaven didn't know where he was. Save for Theo.

"Dude, I really think his Omega killed him," Owen said, repeating what he had been saying for the last four days. "That's what we'll tell the convenors."

"Stop bloody lying to yourself." Braden growled. His body still shook with fury at what they all believed was Saxton's betrayal.

Theo turned to Derrick. "Your thoughts."

Derrick looked at Theo's bruised face.

"Until such time that the search for Saxton's body has ended, I will suspend judgement," he said, his brow rising in challenge.

Theo looked away in disgust. But he knew that Derrick was a by-the-book slayer. Still he couldn't stop the hurt spreading through him of Saxton's betrayal. The slayer he had looked up to. It was only because of that friendship that he kept his mouth shut. And he was going to keep his mouth shut. He still had a sense of fealty towards Saxton not only because Saxton took him under his wing and trained him.

It was because Saxton had also been his friend.

Theo prided himself of being level headed even in the middle of a fight, but he'd lost it four days ago when he couldn't believe that Saxton refused to kill the one thing that held the key to his peace. If he hadn't seen it with his own eyes and had the bruises to prove it, Theo wouldn't have believed that Saxton had fallen in love with his Omega.

Orelle.

She had fooled them all. The fact that Saxton didn't heed Theo's demand to return to Pinehaven clinched it for him. Apollo was lost to them.

Slow rage filled him. An impotent rage that would never go away. He was going to hunt them both down. Because Saxton had been a friend, he was going to die by Theo's hand. Saxton and Orelle. Traitors to their own kind.

He vowed never to go down the same route.

Theo Rennick was never going to give up all that he was.

He would die first before he allowed himself to love a dragon.

†HE END

I hope you enjoyed Saxton's and Orelle's story!
Please consider leaving a short review on your
favourite digital bookstore. Reviews are important for
any author and it would be very much appreciated.

Thank you.

ACKNOWLEDGMENTS

This novella would not have been possible without Denise Kyle who contacted me to ask if I was interested in being a part of the Stoking the Flames anthology. I dedicate this to all of my newly acquired Dragon sisters: Kelli Abell, Solease Baner, Kathi S. Barton, Linda Boulanger, L.J. Garland, Darlene Kuncytes, Andi Lawrencovna, Julia Mills, Tricia Owens, Kate Richards, Kali Willows, Victoria Zak.

Jennifer Stevens, Janka Dustan thank you for being there with me through this whole new paranormal journey. To the ladies who help me spread the word of my books: Debbie Workman, Emily Kirkpatrick, Shirley Bastian, Cheryl Whitty, Christine LaCombe, Barbara Clabeaux, to my readers and new readers and to the bloggers and reviewers who have enjoyed this story, I am forever grateful to all of you for taking a chance on me.

And to my husband and my son, the two most important men in my life. I love you both with all my heart.

ABOUT THE AUTHOR

ISOBELLE CATE is a woman who wears different masks. Mother-writer, wife-professional, scholar-novelist. Currently living in Manchester, she has been drawn to the little known, the secret stories, about the people and the nations: the English, the Irish, the Scots, the Welsh, and those who are now part of these nations whatever their origins. Her vision and passion are fuelled by her interest and background in history and paradoxically, shaped by growing up in a clan steeped in lore, loyalty, and legend.

Isobelle is intrigued by forces that simmer beneath the surface of these cultures, the hidden passions, unsaid desires, and yearnings unfulfilled.

You can contact Isobelle via email:
isobelle@isobellecate.com

Follow Isobelle:

Facebook:
https://www.facebook.com/AuthorIsobelleCate
Twitter: https://twitter.com/Isobelle_Cate
Website: http://www.isobellecate.com/

Other books by
ISOBELLE CATE

The Cynn Cruor Bloodline Series:

Rapture at Midnight
Forever at Midnight
Midnight's Atonement
Midnight' Fate
My Haven, My Midnight
Midnight's Paradox
Midnight's Yule (a novella)
Midnight's Flight (coming soon)

Firebinders Series:

Firebinders: Marek
Firebinders: Rogue (coming soon)

Dragon Hearts Series

Dragonslayer, Dragon Heart
Dragonslayer, Dragon Light (Coming soon)

Paranormal Standalone

Treagar's Redemption
(Woodland Creek Anthology)

Dying To Live

The Second Chances Series
Be Mine
You and I
Take All of Me
Slow Dancing (Coming Soon)

The Mana Series
(Historical Fiction)
Lakam

Other Standalones
Love in Her Dreams

The Club Series
To Have and Hold
Come Fly with Me (with Katherine Rhodes)

24344357R00128

Printed in Poland
by Amazon Fulfillment
Poland Sp. z o.o., Wrocław